THE SWEETEST THING

inside girl

Also by J. Minter:

the insiders
pass it on
take it off
break every rule
hold on tight
girls we love
inside girl

inside girl

THE SWEETEST THING

girl

a novel by J. MINTER

author of the insiders

BLOOMSBURY

for **MEREDITH**

BLOOMSBURY

Copyright © 2007 by J. Minter
and 17th Street Productions, an Alloy company

Published by Bloomsbury U.S.A. Children's Books
175 Fifth Avenue, New York, NY 10010
Distributed to the trade by Holtzbrinck Publishers

Library of Congress Cataloging-in-Publication Data
Minter, J.
The sweetest thing: an inside girl novel / by J. Minter. — 1st U.S. ed.
p.   cm.
Summary: Flan's life is in turmoil when her older siblings decide to act like strict
parents to keep her from becoming out of control like themselves, friends Judith
and Meredith fight over a football player who might just have a crush on Flan
herself, and Sara-Beth tries to find her style.
ISBN-13: 978-1-59990-087-2 • ISBN-10: 1-59990-087-4
[1. Friendship—Fiction. 2. High schools—Fiction. 3. Schools—Fiction. 4. Family
life—New York (State)—Fiction. 5. Dating (Social customs)—Fiction.
6. New York (N.Y.)—Fiction.] I. Title.
PZ7.M67334Swe 2007   [Fic]—dc22   200700889

ALLOYENTERTAINMENT   Produced by Alloy Entertainment
151 West 26th Street, New York, NY 10001

First U.S. Edition 2007
Printed in the U.S.A. by Quebecor World Fairfield
10 9 8 7 6 5 4 3 2 1

For as long as I can remember, my hair has been exactly the same: blond, straight, and just past my shoulders. Once, when I was feeling rebellious, way back in sixth grade, I tried one of those do-it-yourself temporary highlighting kits that turned my hair a horrible orange color. My older sister, Feb, called me the Human Flame for an entire month after that one. But other than that, it's stayed more or less the same, which was fine when I went to my old private school, Mallard Day. But since I started at Stuyvesant, a huge public high school in New York City, six weeks ago, my whole look, including my hair, seemed kind of . . . well, boring.

So when my mom gave me a gift certificate to the Zara Friedich Salon in SoHo, it was clearly a sign that I was due for some big changes. My mom went overboard as usual to compensate for her near-total absenteeism and made the gift certificate for three times as much as was necessary, so rather than spend tons of time alone at the salon getting seriously over-pampered, I decided to treat my new friends Judith and Meredith to haircuts as well.

So there we were, sitting in the vaguely apple-scented salon, when my hair stylist, Monique—a Brooklyn ultra-hipster whose choppy black hair made me feel doubly plain—asked me what I wanted. And that's when I finally decided to quit being cautious and just take the plunge.

"Surprise me."

"Surprise you? Really?" she asked, raising one eyebrow. "The last woman who told me to do that started weeping the moment I finished blow-drying her. Of course, maybe I shouldn't have given a forty-five-year-old hedge-fund manager pink streaks."

On either side of me, Meredith and Judith exchanged nervous glances. I felt an excited flutter in my stomach as I twisted a few damp blond locks around my forefinger. "Do it. I'm ready for a change."

"You won't sue me?"

"Nope. Just do whatever you think would look good," I told her.

Monique smiled and turned up Fall Out Boy. "Okay. If you're sure."

She parted my still-wet hair and began quickly combing it out. All around us, stylish young women were getting their hair trimmed, clipped, chopped, shaped, and folded into tinfoil. I recognized one girl sitting a few chairs down from us from last weekend's *New York Times Magazine*. The salon had sleek chrome furniture, exposed pipes, and funky oversize lightbulbs that hung down from the ceiling on shiny silver chains. I'd felt so ordinary the minute I stepped inside. But now, as Monique made a series of bold sideways snips, I knew I'd come to the perfect place to discover the new me.

"Wow, Flan," Judith whispered as her own stylist trimmed her split ends. "I can't believe you're just letting her choose. You might not even recognize yourself. Are you sure . . . ?" Her eyes widened as a thick chunk of my hair tumbled down to the floor.

Judith is a great friend, but she worries way too much. According to Meredith, who's gone to school with her since kindergarten, Judith's been an over-achiever since the age of six. Apparently she got the second-highest grade on a definitions test and vowed never to let that happen again. She has long blond hair that she likes to flip back over her shoulders when she's making a point in conversation or in an argu-ment for Debate Club, and I can't imagine her ever cutting it off. The thought filled me with a little swell of pride for my daring move.

"Won't Bennett be upset?" she added, as her stylist tilted her head forward so she could fret over her ends.

"I doubt it," I said. Bennett, my boyfriend, is pretty laid-back. We hang out most days after school, and sometimes on weekends, but that day he had a special meeting for the school paper, the *Stuyvesant Spectator*, which he worked on with his friends.

"Oh, come on, Judith," said Meredith. Her damp, dark hair hung in waves down her back. "Guys never notice haircuts. Besides, Flan's making a statement." She smiled at me encouragingly. "Someday I'm going to cut my hair really, really short and then just wear a different wig every day to suit my mood. How fun would that be? I'd have a hipster mullet on Monday, and then on Tuesday I'd have one of those fifties bee-hives that's shaped like a tornado. For days when I have art class, I could wear one of those long, flowy Rapunzel wigs." She frowned. "Although it might get in my oil paints—which is not exactly the kind of 'hairbrush' I like using."

I laughed. Meredith has light brown hair that she usually wears in a ponytail, but I could imagine her doing something crazy like that. Her sense of style and fashion ran in her family. Her mom and grandma own a really cute clothing boutique just down the street from where we were getting our hair cut. The first time I met Meredith, she was wearing a skirt made out of men's ties. That afternoon, she had on a cut-up T-shirt from the '80s with a picture of Blondie on it, and a bunch of chunky bangle bracelets in different colors. She's really into art and photography and poetry, too. She and Judith are so different, it's hard to believe they've been best friends since forever. But I guess best friends don't have to be alike—they just have to get along, and Meredith and Judith go together like strawberries and chocolate. I fit in pretty well with them too. I'd been really lucky to meet such cool people right at the beginning of high school.

"Anyway," Meredith went on, "even if he does notice, Bennett is so into Flan that he won't care. She could come back with a Mohawk, and he'd still be like . . ." Meredith feigned a love-struck expression that caused Judith to shriek with laughter. I blushed.

"Oh, come on, you guys," I said.

"No, Flan, it's really true," Judith agreed. "Bennett's such a great guy. Most of the boys from our school have no clue how to talk to girls!" She made a face. "Kelvin, from biology, was trying to flirt with me the other day. First he told me a dirty joke about USB ports. And then he talked to me about some computer game for twenty minutes while I was trying to finish our lab report. And I said, 'Like I care,' and he kept saying, 'I know!' and then I finally realized he thought I meant I *did* care!"

"Wait. Kelvin—you mean that guy who wheezes when he laughs?" Meredith asked as her stylist spritzed her hair with papaya-scented leave-in conditioner.

Judith sighed. "That's the one. Did I tell you we're lab partners now?"

"Oh no!"

While the two of them went on about Kelvin's creepiness, I found myself thinking about Bennett again. Bennett is older than us—a sophomore—and he's into all kinds of interesting stuff: he reads J. D. Salinger short stories and *Thrasher* magazine and all the latest Tokyopop graphic novels, and always has really well thought out opinions about stuff like why the latest Tarantino movie failed. Unlike clueless boys like Kelvin, Bennett actually talks to me in a way that makes him seem like a friend. He's a great guy to study with and always comes up with the cutest ways to remember names and dates for history class. One time when I was cramming for an algebra test, he made me a whole stack of flash cards with equations on them, and then tied them together with an orange ribbon and a fuzzy, dog-shaped charm that looked just like my Pomeranian, Noodles. Plus, he's adorable. I mean, seriously, he even has dimples. How much cuter could you get?

When I came back down to earth, Meredith and Judith had moved on to one of their favorite topics: their ideal guys.

"I just want somebody who's sensitive." Meredith sighed. A daydreamy look had come into her eyes. "Somebody who believes in truth and beauty—and art. Oh, and books."

"Someone like . . . Jules?!" Judith laughed. Meredith had a thing for one of Bennett's friends, which Judith found totally hilarious. Okay, so maybe Jules wasn't the hottest guy I'd ever seen, but he was really tall and nice, and when he told one of his funny stories, he instantly became the life of the party. I always figured he and Meredith would get together, just because they both did their own thing and dressed like no one else at Stuy. Jules wore vintage suit jackets and old Hawaiian shirts, and one time he even wore a fedora complete with a peacock feather to a party.

"Oh no, I'm so over him," she said with a dismissive

wave of her hand. "Now I've got my eye on someone in my honors freshman English class."

"Really?" Judith raised her voice over the noise of her stylist's hair-dryer. "When did this happen?"

"Yesterday." Meredith met my eyes in the salon's mirror. "We were reading Shakespeare's sonnets in class, and when it got to be his turn, Mr. Welninski told him to put feeling into it, and . . . wow. I've never heard anything so beautiful. It was like the Bard himself was there in the room with us."

"So what does this bard look like?" Judith inspected the back of her hair in the mirror her stylist had handed her. "That looks great. Can you flatiron it for me, please?"

"Well, this isn't why I like him, of course, but he does happen to be *gorgeous*."

Judith clapped her hands, and I giggled.

"Seriously. He's got silver moons for eyes. And he's all athletic and chiseled looking—like one of those statues of Hercules from ancient Rome."

"Who *is* this guy?" I demanded. "I think I'd remember if I saw someone like that walking around Stuy."

"His name is Adam McGregor." Meredith shut her eyes blissfully as her stylist started to blow her out, her hair dancing around her face in the warm air.

I don't think Meredith heard Judith gasp over the buzz of the dryer. But I did.

"What's wrong?" I asked her.

Meredith opened her eyes again. Judith was staring at her, a horrified look on her face.

"What?" Meredith looked confused.

"Oh no, not again!" Judith cried. Suddenly a shocked, knowing expression crept over Meredith's face.

"Again, what?" I asked, looking back and forth between them, totally lost. The problem with becoming friends with two people who've known each forever is that I sometimes have no idea what they're talking about.

"Stop moving your head." Monique steadied my half-styled head with one hand and brandished a pair of scissors in the other.

"Adam McGregor the football player?" asked Judith. "The Josh Hartnett lookalike with curly brown hair?"

Meredith nodded solemnly and covered her face with her hands in despair.

"That guy?" I laughed. "Meredith, he's in bio with me, and he's definitely not sensitive. He just sits in the back of the class with all his teammates, flicking pencils at one another. The last time the teacher called on him, he was like, 'Ummm . . . my concussion is acting up, can you repeat the question?'"

"Oh, that's not true at all. He's super smart and totally witty." Judith kicked her legs under her black smock. "But that's not the problem."

"The problem is . . ." Meredith began.

"We both like him!" they wailed in unison. Several people in the salon turned to look our way. The *New York Times Magazine* model clucked her tongue disapprovingly as she turned the page of the *W* she was reading.

I still felt confused. How could they both like him when this was the first time they'd ever mentioned him? "Are you sure?" I asked. "How well do you even know him?"

Meredith moaned, ignoring my question. "And the worst part is that this exact thing happened when we were in sixth grade. It was *awful*. We almost stopped being friends over it."

Judith lowered her voice, even though her stylist had wandered off to find a wide-toothed comb and no one was really trying to overhear. "See, Meredith and I had this friend, Fiona, who lived in Park Slope, and during the summer we'd go out there to tan up on her roof. Fiona's brother was absolutely the cutest guy we'd ever seen in our lives, and we were both totally, totally in love with him."

Meredith pressed one hand to her heart over her black smock. "I still dream about him sometimes. Tall and handsome, with coal black, smoldering eyes."

"He was a hunk," Judith put in bluntly.

"Hunk?" I asked. Did anybody besides my mom still use that word?

"Yeah, totally. Anyway, all that summer, we competed over him—buying new swimsuits every week, wearing makeup over our suntan lotion, trying to talk to him, even." She grinned, despite herself. "Back then we never, ever talked to the guys we liked."

"Huh." I suppressed a smile. Meredith and Judith still got serious cases of the giggles around boys, but I figured it was probably best to not point that out. Behind me Monique finally set down her scissors and picked up her blow-dryer. She turned it on low.

"It got kind of out of control," Meredith went on. "Finally, one day, on the way over to their house, Judith said she was going to ask him out on a date, and there was nothing I could do to stop her. So I told her if she tried anything, I'd tell him she still slept with her blanky."

"I can't believe you did that," Judith broke in. I

couldn't tell if she was kidding or not—her voice was somewhere in between joking and serious.

"Anyhow," Meredith continued, "by the time we got to Fiona's, we were both about to explode—which we did as soon as we saw Tony playing a video game in the living room. We just started screaming at each other in front of everyone. Tony hadn't known that we liked him, and I guess he was kind of freaked out, because he ran away and locked himself in his room." Meredith looked over at me sheepishly. "He wouldn't come out till we went back to Manhattan. We never saw him again."

"Wow." It was kind of hard to imagine Meredith and Judith fighting. The whole time I'd known them, they'd been practically inseparable. But from the expressions on their faces, I could tell the Tony incident had been a huge deal.

"That's why we're never going to let that happen again." Judith gave Meredith a sharp look that bordered on a glare. "No guy's worth *that*."

"No, definitely not," Meredith said emphatically. She twisted an orange bangle bracelet around her wrist. "We swore never to let another guy come between us."

"Okay," Monique cut in, "you're done!" I'd been so caught up listening to Judith and Meredith that I'd hardly paid attention to what Monique was doing to my hair. But when I looked up and saw my reflection in the mirror, I let out a shriek.

It was like Monique had looked into the future and seen an older, cooler me. She'd moved my part to the left, and had cut sleek side-swept bangs across my forehead. She had kept my hair essentially the same length, but rather than just hanging straight across, it now hung in choppy layers around my shoulders. It looked amazing—sophisticated and stylish, and totally perfect for the new me.

Even though Meredith was probably right about boys never noticing haircuts, I still couldn't wait for Bennett to see it. He's really perceptive, and he'd spent so much time with me lately, I figured he'd have to notice right away . . . right?

Well, as I soon found out, that wasn't exactly true.

*I*t may not be Nobu, but Stuyvesant's cafeteria is beautiful. It's more like a private dining room you'd find in a museum than in a regular high school, and you can see the Hudson River from all the windows. Meredith, Judith, and I eat lunch there almost every day. But that Monday Judith had a Debate Club prep session, and Meredith, who was working on costumes for the school's annual musical, had to go to a cast-and-crew pizza party behind the stage in the auditorium. It was actually the perfect day for them to be busy, though, because between getting my haircut and then showing it off to my family the night before and then staring at it in the mirror in my bathroom, I hadn't had time to finish reading my English assignment.

I was looking forward to finding a quiet table in the corner, but when I walked through the cafeteria doors, the entire place was in an uproar. It was even more chaotic than on Falafel Day. Cheerful, football-themed decorations hung from every surface in the room. The coffered ceiling was covered with big loops of crepe paper in red and blue—the team colors—and an enormous inflatable football was suspended over the food line. A giant full-color poster plastered on the far wall advertised the big football game against Brooklyn Tech on Saturday at the Columbia University stadium, while a bunch of smaller ones reminded students about the pep rally that afternoon. I'd completely forgotten about the rally. I've never been a big fan of school sports—I played volleyball in seventh grade, but that was because we didn't have to take gym if we did an extracurricular. Plus, Mallard Day didn't really have sports teams that were competitive with other schools. So the crazy excitement sweeping through Stuy was a new thing for me.

After getting my food—a cucumber-and-hummus sandwich with a bottle of green tea—I shouldered past a bunch of girls wearing cheerleading outfits and found a table over by the window. I should have been reading my English assignment as I munched on my sandwich and sipped my tea, but instead I looked out over the water. I couldn't help but worry about what Meredith and Judith had said about Adam yesterday.

Even though they said they would never let a boy come between them again, how would they be able to forget about Adam when the whole school seemed to have football fever? Adam was probably one of those guys who relished having girls fall all over him so he could brag about it to his teammates. It would never even occur to him that there were real friendships at stake. I mean, I really had seen him in class, and he just wasn't a cool guy at all.

Just then, Adam McGregor and his football buddies burst into the cafeteria, wearing white button-down shirts and matching red-and-blue striped ties. Now even if I had wanted to finish my homework rather than ruminate about Adam and his cocky ways, I wouldn't have been able to. Because the minute the football players ran in, about half the lunchroom jumped up and cheered. The boys grinned like crazy as they went through the food line, piling their trays full of carbs and electric blue Gatorade.

I shook my head in disbelief. This was New York, cultural center of the world, home of the Met and the Guggenheim. Getting riled up about the Yankees is one thing, but this was *high school* football. Who did these guys think they were?

Sure, some of them weren't terrible looking. I mean, it wasn't like they were mathletes, so they were all in pretty good shape, if a little bulked up for my taste. And yeah, Adam had the sort of clean-cut, all-American look you might see in a J. Crew catalog. But it didn't seem right that the school rearranged classes to worship football players at a pep rally when people like Bennett, who worked on the school paper, barely got to use the Xerox machine.

It was just my luck that, of all the tables still open, Adam and his friends decided to take over the one next to mine. As they clattered trays down one after the other and punched one another in the shoulder, I sighed and decided that I, for one, wasn't going to pay them any attention. I pulled my English text-book out of my bag and opened it to the section we were going to have a quiz on next period, a short story from forever ago by this guy named O. Henry, like the candy bar. Maybe he was some eccentric chocolate tycoon like Willy Wonka who wrote in his spare time.

I sighed again and, forcing myself to ignore the hoots and backslaps coming from the next table, started to read. The story was called "The Gift of the Magi," and it turned out to be about a young married couple living in the city who were too poor to buy each other Christmas presents. I tried to get into it, but when I reached the bottom of the first page, I realized I wasn't really paying attention to the words in front of me.

Adam and his teammates kept laughing and shouting to one another, and I was getting more and more annoyed. How rude was it to come into a public place like this and treat it like your own private VIP room? Maybe they all had concussions or whatever, but some of us had to study.

I guess I had been shooting Adam quite a few annoyed glances, because after a couple of minutes, I noticed he was looking my way. I quickly stared down at my book and tried to hide my irritated expression, but it was too late. When I slowly raised my eyes again, he was already standing up and coming over toward me.

Adam is about six foot three, with an athletic build. I'd always thought big guys like him were plodding and clumsy. But the way he skirted through the maze of scratched-up wooden chairs as he walked toward me made him seem almost like an acrobat or gymnast. Still, I wasn't overly impressed. He was that generic type of good looking, with no personality in his face, nothing cool and quirky and unique like Bennett, or even my old boyfriend Jonathan. And I totally disagreed with Judith—he didn't look a thing like Josh Hartnett, unless you counted the broad shoulders.

Which I didn't. When he reached my table, he smiled and pulled out a chair across from me, then sat down on the very edge, like he was only going to stay for a second.

"Sorry about the noise," he said, in that low, clear voice Meredith had thought was so perfect for reading poetry. He nodded at my English textbook. "It must be annoying if you're trying to study. We're just excited to kick off the season. I hope you can forgive us."

"Well, it's just—" But as I looked at his good-natured grin, I could feel my irritation begin to melt away. I wanted to say, *Yes, you're being ridiculously loud,* but somehow what came out of my mouth was, "Oh, it's fine. Don't worry about it."

"What's that you're reading?" As he reached across the table to grab my book, I noticed he was wearing a vintage, blue-faced Breitling watch, kind of like the one my brother's crazy friend Mickey Pardo always wears. It was surprising, because I'd pegged him as a run-of-the-mill Hilfiger or Fossil kind of guy.

"Just a short story for English class next period." I hoped he would get the hint from my short answer that I wanted my book back.

"I'm in Welninski's section," he said, completely oblivious to my desire for him to leave. His nose crinkled as he glanced at the first page of the O. Henry story. "We started off with the poetry unit, but I read ahead a little." He tapped the page with one finger. "I liked this story."

"You did?" A football player reading ahead?

"Sure. O. Henry's stuff is pretty entertaining. He's no Hemingway, but his endings are great. They're always a little twisted. You finish this one yet?"

"We're having a quiz on it today, and I didn't really get a chance to study," I admitted. "I was working on the bio worksheets all night." Someone on the food line dropped a ceramic bowl with a clatter. Several people stood up and clapped as the red-faced girl bent to gather the broken shards.

"Don't remind me." Adam rolled his eyes, and I noticed that Meredith had been wrong. There in the sunlight, I could see that his eyes weren't silver moons, like she'd said. They were green, and if I were being poetic and flowery like her, I might've even said they were chartreuse, the same color as my warmest, fuzziest cardigan sweater.

"That class is impossible." Adam ran his finger along a wide groove in the wooden table and looked at me earnestly. "I don't know how I'm going to survive the semester. I can barely stay on top of all the reading, let alone understand it. Mitochondria, chlorophyll—it's like learning another language."

"It's confusing at first, but if you have someone explain it well, it's actually kind of easy," I remarked, thinking of Bennett and his helpful flash cards.

Adam's chair squeaked as he leaned back and balanced the chair on its two back legs. "Easy? Well, maybe you could help me, then."

"Oh—" Startled, I frantically scrolled through a mental list of people other than Meredith or Judith who could walk Adam through the intricacies of the Krebs cycle. I drew a blank, but then to my surprise, I heard myself say, "Um, I'm not an expert or anything, but I could try."

"Great!" He slid the English book back across the table to me and stood up. "There's only five minutes left before lunch ends—I should let you get back to your story. I'm warning you, though, it's kind of a heartbreaker."

Five minutes? I couldn't believe I had been talking to Adam for so long. "I have a quiz on this next period and I'm never going to finish in time. Can you just quickly tell me what happens?"

He squinted at me. "I don't want to ruin the ending for you."

"No, really, it's okay. I'd rather pass than have the ending be a surprise."

He leaned forward on the table like he was telling

me a secret. "You know how the guy has the watch he loves? And the woman has the beautiful long hair?"

I nodded. I'd read that far at least.

"Well, he sells his watch to buy her these fancy combs. Meanwhile, she decides to get him this expensive watch chain, but to pay the jewelry store guy she has to sell her hair."

"That's terrible!" I exclaimed.

"Nah, it's romantic—they both gave up something they loved to make each other happy. And who knows? Maybe her hair was even cuter after the cut. Like yours." He winked as he turned to walk back to his table. "It's a good look for you, Flan."

I couldn't believe he'd noticed. Apparently Adam had been paying more attention to me—and my hair—than to the mitochondria. I realized I was grinning from ear to ear. But before I had a chance to recover, someone reached around from behind me and covered my eyes with their hands.

Chapter 3

migod!" I gasped, twisting around in my seat. "Bennett! I thought you had a meeting for the paper."

My heart was racing. Had he overheard my conversation with Adam? All that talk about romance and my hair being cute could *definitely* be misinterpreted. But Bennett just plopped down in the chair next to me and took a bite out of his red-and-green McIntosh apple.

"I wanted to see you, so I took off early." He grinned, showing the chipped front tooth he'd gotten when his rowboat once capsized in the Central Park lake.

I love Bennett's smile. It makes him look more genuine somehow, maybe because, without it, he'd just be too perfectly adorable. His dirty blond hair is long and kind of tousled looking, like he's in a band or going surfing, and he has a light dusting of freckles

23

just across the bridge of his nose. That afternoon, he was wearing a Weezer T-shirt over a gray long-sleeved waffle shirt. His worn Diesel jeans were fraying at the cuffs.

"Was that the new quarterback?" Bennett asked, jerking his head in the direction of Adam's table. So he *had* noticed me talking to Adam.

"Yeah, he's in my bio class." I tried to keep my voice even and innocent sounding. I mean, I hadn't done anything wrong, but somehow I didn't want Bennett to know that I might be tutoring a tall, athletic guy who liked my new haircut. Bennett nodded distractedly and unwrapped the most unappetizing-looking liverwurst-and-mustard sandwich I'd ever seen.

"Hey, listen," Bennett said between bites. "I'm writing the film review next week. Want to come see a Russian movie about malevolent clones?"

"Clones?" Bennett was only a sophomore, but he was already one of the best reporters for the *Stuyvesant Spectator*. He took his journalistic duties seriously, particularly his film reviews. In the month we'd been dating, I'd sat in tons of darkened movies theaters with him, watching everything from romantic comedies about forty-year-olds meeting each other on MySpace to an action movie about man-eating catfish. Bennett referred to that one as *Freshwater Jaws*. Sometimes Meredith and Judith came along as well, and we would all go out for coffee or ice cream afterward and make fun of the cheesy sets and do our own renditions of the more poorly acted scenes. Meredith does a great mangled jellyfish. It was fun to sit in the theater with Bennett's arm around my shoulders, but a lot of the movies we saw weren't exactly my style. I prefer old classics from the '40s, like *Casablanca* and *His Girl Friday*, with their snappy dialogue and soft-focus kisses.

Bennett noted my hesitation and reached out to touch my knee. "How about this: we do evil clones next week, and the week after we'll go to the special midnight showing of *All About Eve* at the Angelika?"

"Seriously?" *All About Eve* is one of my favorite movies ever. It's hilarious, and, based on the stories my best friend, actress Sara-Beth Benny, tells me, all the conniving and fighting between the actresses is pretty true to life. And it was perfect—clones for Bennett, and Bette Davis for me. Plus, I love the Angelika. It's the only theater I've been to where you can buy fresh chocolate chip cookies with pecans instead of peanut M&M's. I'd eaten bags and bags of M&M's in the last month and was excited for the cookies. I thought of the couple from the O. Henry story, how they each gave up something to make the other happy, and bumped Bennett's shoulder affectionately.

Just then the lunch bell rang, and we scrambled to finish our sandwiches. When I stood up and stuffed my English book into my brown suede schoolbag, he put his hand on my shoulder and squinted a little.

"Hey, you look kind of different." He looked me up and down carefully. All around us chairs scraped against the scuffed wood floor as students got up to toss their lunches in garbage cans and shuffle out of the cafeteria. "Are you wearing a new shirt or something?"

Was it possible that not one but two boys had noticed my new hairdo? Either I looked really hot, or they were way more observant than Meredith gave them credit for. "Guess again," I said with a teasing smile.

"New makeup? It's not a piercing, that's obvious. . . ." Bennett put both hands on the back of his chair and studied me.

I played with the ends of my newly shorn hair and narrowed my eyes. It bothered me a little that he couldn't see what was right in front of him, especially when Adam, who barely knew me, had noticed right away. "Well, listen, if you don't know, I'm not going to tell you."

Bennett shrugged. "Okay—I have to run, but I know I'll figure it out by the end of the day!"

He kissed me on the cheek, then wove his way through the crowded cafeteria to the exit. I started to follow him, but for some reason I stopped and glanced back at the table where Adam was sitting. He was still there, and, as all his friends picked up their trays and backpacks, his eyes met mine. Maybe Meredith and Judith had some sort of contagious Adam-obsession disease, because, for just a second, I couldn't take my eyes off him.

his is so intense!" Judith exclaimed, grabbing my hand to lead me up the bleachers at the pep rally later that afternoon. Judith, Meredith, and I had met outside the old gym at the beginning of seventh period so we could sit together at the mandatory, schoolwide event. Stuy actually has two gyms, which is pretty amazing for a school in downtown Manhattan. My old private school didn't even have one. Instead, we played four-square and volleyball in the little courtyard outside, and when we had all-school assemblies, we usually just rented out the ballroom at the Sherry-Netherland Hotel down the street.

The old gym is really pretty—it has big skylights that flood the room with sunshine, and the image of Pegleg Pete, our school mascot, is laid out in tiles on the floor. And like the cafeteria, it was brightly decorated for the start of football season. Big banners still shining with wet paint hung from the cinder-block walls, and the dance squad was roving around, throwing out fistfuls of confetti shaped like tiny red and blue footballs.

Almost in spite of myself, I felt a tremor of excitement run through me. It was my first ever pep rally, and the whole gym seemed to buzz with energy. It's funny—Stuy has a reputation for being a really academic school, but people here definitely had school spirit. A bunch of girls had tied their hair back with red and blue ribbons, and a lot of students had changed into Stuyvesant sweatshirts, T-shirts, jackets—you name it. My brown Mia flats and lemon yellow tank with little chiffon ruffles had looked cute when I left the house that morning, but now, in this sea of red and blue, I felt a little bit out of place.

Meredith, Judith, and I finally found seats at the top of the bleachers. The school band was playing the fight song at top volume, and it was so loud the metal bench vibrated beneath us. I could barely hear what my friends were saying, but the way their eyes were scanning the crowd gave me the sinking suspicion that they were desperately trying to find Adam. I spotted a bewildered-looking Bennett as he walked into the gym and waved him up to our seats. He bounded up the bleachers behind three guys who had painted their faces school colors.

Bennett threw his messenger bag at my feet and shook his head in disgust. "Wow. That's just too much," he said, pointing at the red-and-blue guys. One of them let out a whoop and bobbed his head violently in time to the music. "It's just a rally—not even an actual game!"

"I guess they went a little overboard," I said, although I was kind of wishing I'd worn my red cashmere sweater over my jeans.

"Hey—is it okay if we sit with you guys?" Jules and Eric, one of Bennett's friends whom Judith had had a crush on pre-Adam, were standing at the end of our aisle, looking sort of awkward. They weren't wearing school colors either, but Jules looked cute in his khakis and vintage bowling shirt that had a little martini glass on the pocket.

"Hey, Meredith." He smiled at her, his eyes crinkling sweetly behind his black-framed glasses.

"Oh, hi, Jules." Meredith barely even glanced at him as she and Judith scooted down to make room for them. I could tell by the way he looked at her that he was a little disappointed by her lukewarm greeting. Like Judith's, her eyes were trained on the big double doors in the back of the gym that led to the football locker room.

"Pep rallies are beyond pointless," Eric groaned, reaching across my lap to bump fists with Bennett. According to Judith, Eric is the hottest guy in the sophomore class, but he can definitely rub me the wrong way. He's always bragging about the super-stylish people he knows and the awesome clubs he's been to—even though he's actually barely been any-where—and at some point he decided he's going to be the next big male model. He's always acting really vain and spritzing himself with antiseptic-smelling cologne. But since he was friends with Bennett, I decided to try my best to be nice to him. If Bennett could handle Meredith and Judith acting nuts—giggling like crazy and then suddenly shooting suspicious glances at each other, like they were doing right now—I could easily put up with a little bit of Eric's pretension.

"Hi, Flan." Eric offered his hand for me to shake. The second I let go, he doused his palm in hand-sanitizer. "Sorry," he said. "I have an audition for another hand-modeling job, and I just can't be too careful."

"That's . . . great," I said, trying to restrain myself from smacking his perfect fingers with a heavy book.

"Hey, man." Bennett and Jules exchanged some kind of complicated handshake. "You have those movie stills for me for *Russian Clones*?"

Jules works on the school paper with Bennett, doing photography and graphic design stuff.

"Sure thing. I'll e-mail them to you this afternoon," he said. But he kept glancing over his shoulder at Meredith, who was straining to see past Judith down to the floor. "Hey, Meredith, I'm surprised you're here. I thought you might ditch out because you don't like sports."

"She doesn't," Judith told him. Meredith looked at her sharply. "Well, no offense, Meredith, but it's true. You're not exactly into football."

"I like football," Meredith exclaimed. "I liked that movie *Jerry Maguire*. There's a football player in that."

"That's so not the same as watching an actual game." Judith pulled a red-and-blue scarf out of her backpack with a flourish and swung it loosely around her neck.

Meredith stared at the scarf, as if willing it to disappear.

Just then, the new Gwen Stefani song burst from the loud speakers, and the pom-pom squad began dancing, signaling the start of the pep rally. Gwen Stefani usually irritates me, but the cheerleaders' dance moves were really athletic and cute, almost like ballet, and it was fun cheering for them along with the rest of the school. And by "the rest of the school," I mean everybody but Bennett and his friends, because they were making fun of just about everything by that point.

"Is that girl a soloist, or is she just five steps behind?" asked Jules.

Bennett laughed. "Maybe it's an interpretive dance. 'This is the part where I reject my mother's dream of medical school and pick up the pom-poms instead.'"

"Oh, come on, guys," I said. "That takes real athletic ability. Give them a break."

Eric took out a salad and started eating. Bennett and Jules turned and stared at him. "What?" he asked. "I need to eat greens every twenty minutes, or I'll lose my skin tone."

Suddenly Meredith and Judith jumped to their feet, and the rest of the school was up about two seconds later, waving banners and yelling like crazy. The football players were running into the gym, throwing footballs back and forth. When Adam jogged in at the back of the line, the entire gym began chanting, "McGregor! McGregor!" Down there, under the lights of the gym, he looked graceful and capable, like he was totally destined to lead our team to victory.

"Can you believe that guy's only a freshman?"

asked Jules, trying to make conversation with Meredith. "He must be one hell of a player."

"Yeah." She and Judith sighed dreamily. From the love-struck expressions on their faces, it was clear their crushes weren't going away anytime soon. As the football team lined up and Adam flashed the crowd a smile that was charming, friendly, and totally at ease, I had to admit that I couldn't really blame them.

Chapter 5

After school I walked home to my town house on Perry Street in Greenwich Village, and with each step I took I got more and more worried about the whole Adam situation. Even if I was starting to understand why Meredith and Judith liked him, their weird competitiveness at the pep rally was definitely a bad sign. Their fight over Tony had sounded so awful, and that was back in middle school when they barely even saw the guy. But now they both had classes with Adam and saw him on a daily basis. What would happen if one of them ended up going out with him? Would they really just throw away their friendship over some guy? Maybe I was jumping the gun a little with all my worries, but hanging out with Meredith and Judith had made my transition to Stuy so fun and easy. I didn't want anything to come between us, and I definitely didn't want to ever have to choose one of

35

them as a friend over the other. I had worked myself into a state of total anxiety by the time I reached my block, and I realized I really needed to talk to someone about it all. So instead of scaling the steps to my own house, I walked one house further and rang the buzzer. It was time to pay a visit to my best friend, Sara-Beth Benny.

Unless you've been living in a bomb shelter since the late '80s, you've heard of Sara-Beth Benny. She was the adorable star child of the hit show *Mike's Princesses,* and since then, she's been in a bunch of movies and on the covers of even more magazines. She's totally terrified of the paparazzi. Over the years, she's built up this whole collection of wigs and costumes and giant sunglasses to hide behind, and when we go out she's always ducking behind parked cars, furniture, and potted plants.

Back in September SBB moved out of her Upper East Side apartment because photographers kept ambushing her there and driving her even crazier. But before she finally moved into the enormous brownstone right next to mine, she'd been living at my house, apartment-hunting and hiding from the paparazzi. SBB has been my best friend for a while now, but as much as I love her, I have to admit it was pretty stressful sharing a bedroom with her. It's so much more fun to have her next door—now I can just pop on over whenever I want to chat or just catch up on the details of her too-fabulous, too-exciting life.

When SBB's door finally swung open, an exhausted-looking man in dirty coveralls greeted me gruffly. "You Flan?" I nodded. He gestured over one shoulder with a paintbrush whose bristles were stained a metallic gold. "Her Majesty's in there."

"Thanks." I hurried past him into the living room.

"Oh. My. God." Ever since she moved in, Sara-Beth had been kind of neurotic about decorating her new town house, but she had taken it to an entirely new level. The downstairs looked more like a Lower East Side hookah bar at midnight than a home. The walls were covered with dark, almost black wood paneling, and huge crimson velvet festoons hung from the ceiling down over the windows. The couches that had been there just two days ago were gone, and instead large silk pillows with elaborate embroidery and enormous tassels were positioned at jaunty angles around the room. The trim around the windows and wainscoting at the top of the ceiling had been painted gold, and an enormous bronze statue of a jaguar stood in the far-left corner of the room, its fangs bared and its jeweled, ruby-red eyes flashing.

I coughed and squinted. A huge cone of incense

was burning on a hammered brass tray, and the smoke was curling through every inch of air in the room. The whole place made me think of the caterpillar's mushroom from Alice in Wonderland. What kind of crazy rabbit hole had I fallen through to get here?

"Sara-Beth?" I called weakly, trying to get some oxygen. "You in here?"

Somewhere upstairs a gong sounded, and I watched Sara-Beth slowly descend the circular staircase leading into the living room. She was wearing a dark blue silk robe stitched with golden starbursts, and matching silk pants. Little bells hung at the ends of her sleeves, jingling as she walked. Her plum-colored lipstick matched the pillow she chose to sit down on. I pulled over a dark green one and flopped down next to her.

"Flan, sweetie!! Your new haircut is amazing! It reminds me of a dream I just had," Sara-Beth exclaimed.

"Thanks! But Sara-Beth," I said, choking slightly on the thick, incense-laden air, "what on earth is going on? What happened to your furniture?"

"Oh, furniture is so constrictive." Sara-Beth swatted at the incense smoke billowing toward her. "When I was out looking for a new sofa, I met Nada. She showed me a better way."

"Nada?" As in, Nada ounce of taste? This was getting stranger all the time. Next Sara-Beth would be telling me this lady had a dog named Zilch.

"Isn't that a pretty name? She told me it means 'drinker of the moon.'" Sara-Beth smiled. "Anyway, she's my new designer. They've still got a lot of work to do, but this house is going to be a home in no time."

I glanced around and nodded slowly. I didn't want to say it, but her place looked more like an opium den than anything I'd want for a house. Before I had time to come up with a compliment about the new decorations, a woman in a purple velvet kimono came in, pushing a clothes rack hung with all kinds of heavy, fringey fabrics.

"Oh, Nada! There you are. We were just talking about you."

Nada smiled, her sleeves jingling like Sara-Beth's. She was about my mom's age, with long, frizzy brown and gray hair that almost reached her waist. Her shiny gray satin slippers tapered to a point at the toes and then curved up, like elf shoes.

"These are for the wall hangings and pillows," said Nada, pointing at the fabrics at the front of the rack. "The rest are for your tailor."

"Your tailor?" I asked.

Sara-Beth turned to me eagerly. "Isn't it wonderful, Flan! I'm going to match the house. It'll be really good for my chi."

"Um . . . like in the *Sound of Music,* when the kids wear outfits made out of curtains?" I hoped I sounded supportive.

Sara-Beth clapped her hands. "Yes, exactly! Oh, Flan, I knew you'd understand. Isn't Nada a genius?"

Nada smiled and smoothed her hair back. I noticed she had a New Age pyramid tattooed on her wrist. "I like to share my energies with others however I can. The home should be an extension of your aura, and anything that obstructs the vibrations—"

Sara-Beth smiled vaguely and waved her away. Nada looked somewhat downcast as she wheeled the rack back out of the room, jingling as she went. The minute she was gone, Sara-Beth collapsed backward onto two more pillows.

"All this remodeling is making me *insane,*" she moaned. "You have no idea what it's like, having people in your house all the time, moving your stuff around. It reminds me of *Mike's Princesse*s, when those horrible, horrible soundmen would string up microphones all over my kitchen and spy on my conversations."

"You mean the kitchen on the *Mike's Princesses* set?"

"Well, yes, but it was the only kitchen I'd ever *known*." Sara-Beth's eyes filled with tears. "Couldn't they allow a girl a little privacy?"

I blinked, but fortunately Sara-Beth recovered before I had time to respond."Anyway, I'm just so relieved to see you. Tell me," she begged, grabbing my arm, "what's happening out there in the real world? How's . . . everything? How's . . . school?"

"School's okay." I stretched my legs out onto a dusty pink pillow. "I actually wanted to talk to you about Meredith and Judith, though."

"Oh, Meredith and Judith!" Sara-Beth wriggled with delight. "They're so adorable. The happy one and the smart one. Like Tweedledum and Tweedledee. Let's all hang out soon!!"

"Definitely." I nodded. "But yesterday when we were at the salon, Meredith was talking about this guy she likes, Adam—but then it turned out that Judith likes him, too. They're pretending it's okay, but I'm just worried the whole thing will spiral out of control, that they'll get into a huge fight and none of us will be friends any more," I said in a rush.

Sara-Beth slapped her hands to her face in mock horror, and I couldn't help but start cracking up. The situation did sound pretty ridiculous and overblown when I said it out loud.

"I guess I'm worrying about it too much," I admitted. "It's just that they're my only real friends at Stuy. Plus, something like this happened to them before, where they fought over the same guy and practically killed each other. So I guess I'm just scared that history will repeat itself."

Sara-Beth nodded sagely, her dangly gold earrings swinging around her face. "Oh, Flan, girls can be so silly. When I was your age, I was always getting into fights with my friends."

"Really?"

"Of course! My friend Ashleigh-Ann Martin and I were always trying to get the same parts in movies and TV. If I went in to try out for a new pilot, she'd be there too, flirting with the casting assistant. If my agent was talking to some up-and-coming director, then her agent was on the other line. For a while there, we got really competitive. It almost ruined our friendship when I got the lead in *Blennophobia* and they accidentally assigned her to the catering crew." Sara-Beth giggled at the memory.

"So what did you do?" I asked, running my fingers over the rough gold braiding that lined the seams of my pillow.

"Well, we finally made a deal. If there was a project we both really, really wanted"—Sara-Beth leaned forward conspiratorially—"then neither of us would try to get it."

"Really? Neither of you?"

"Nope. Because if one of us got it, then we couldn't be friends anymore, and neither of us would be happy."

"Wow." I pushed my hair behind my ear. "I mean, Meredith and Judith said they wouldn't let a boy come between them again, but they just seemed so upset . . . and into him."

"You can borrow my solution if you want. Set an official rule like I did with Ashleigh-Ann and then really make them stick to that promise."

"Do you think they'd agree to it?"

"Probably. How do you feel about facing west? Are we facing west right now? Nada says we all think most clearly when we're facing west."

I grinned and leaned over to give her an impulsive hug. "You're such a good friend, Sara-Beth. You're definitely facing west."

"Well, I try." She crossed her arms, making the bells at the ends of her sleeves jingle, and nodded once, like a genie granting a wish. "Now it's your turn to give me some advice."

"Shoot."

She poked me in the shoulder with one bony

finger. "What do you think of the new decorations? I mean really?"

I glanced around. "Well . . ."

"Please, *please* be honest." Sara-Beth's breath picked up, which was always a good hint that if I wasn't careful, she might start to cry.

"Okay." I plucked at the tassel attached to my pillow. "It's nice and everything, but I guess it's just not—"

"Not what?"

"Well, it's not really you."

Sara-Beth's eyes got wide, and for a second I thought it was time for the waterworks. But instead she just sighed.

"I *know*." She flopped down onto her elbows and balanced her chin in her hands. For a minute, she looked totally mournful, but then a new thought occurred to her and she brightened up again. "Oh well. I guess I'll know me when I see it, right?"

"Oh, *definitely*," I said. But I don't think either of us knew that we might not see the real her for *quite* some time.

Chapter 6

When I left Sara-Beth's place around five thirty, I was expecting to go home, run up the stairs to my bedroom, and stay holed up there till dinnertime, working on homework until I got so bored I had no choice but to go on IM and talk to all my friends about how much stuff I still had to do. But the minute I swung the front door in on its hinges, I knew something was wrong. For one thing, all the lights were on, and at my house, the only time all the lights are on is at four o'clock in the morning when one of my brother's parties has just ended and he wants to survey the damage. I could also hear the sounds of pots and pans clattering on the stove in the kitchen, which didn't really make any sense, since most of our meals go directly from delivery containers onto china plates. But the weirdest thing of all was how clean it was.

Our house isn't usually that dirty—we have a

cleaning lady, Sveta, who comes in once a week to beat the couch cushions with a stick and curse our filthy ways in Russian—but even after she leaves it's hardly spotless. There's always a splash of red wine on the carpet (usually courtesy of my sister, Feb), or a pile of dirty laundry, or tire marks on the furniture (which tends to happen when Patch's friend Mickey rides his Vespa through our living room). But that day, it was spotless. I could still see the tracks from the vacuum cleaner all across the tan woven rug my parents had brought back from their last trip to Malaysia.

"Mom?" I called hesitantly. "Dad?"

"Flanny! You're home!" Feb sang out, appearing in the doorway to the kitchen. I was so surprised I dropped my schoolbag. It landed with a loud *thunk* on the floor. Feb's sense of style is pretty much the opposite of conservative—she has short black hair, a fondness for clumpy mascara, and a whole closetful of sequined sheath dresses. I'm more likely to see her dancing in a pair of four-inch Roger Vivier stilettos than padding around our apartment in Kate Spade flats. But that day her transformation was even more shocking than that of Sara-Beth Benny's apartment. Here stood my wild big sister in a cute little blue-checked apron. A matching checked headband held back her hair, which she had flipped out at the ends. Her nails were painted powder pink, and in her left hand was a large wooden spoon stained with something red. Looking back, I guess it was probably tomato sauce, but at the time, I thought it must be blood from when she'd beaned the *real* February over the head, because there was no way my real big sister was actually cooking dinner.

"Heya," she cooed adorably, taking a sip from the martini glass she held, less surprisingly, in the other hand. "How was your day at school?"

"All . . . right . . ." I said slowly, trying to figure out exactly what was going on. Feb might ask me questions like, "I know you weren't there, but have you heard what happened after I passed out?" or, "Where the hell did you put those aspirin?" but never questions about school. Certain kinds of sisterly chitchats just weren't her cup of . . . tea.

"Come on into the kitchen." She beckoned with the wooden spoon. "I've been baking cookies!"

I cautiously followed her to the kitchen, where I was astonished to find our usually barren stainless-steel counters littered with evidence that someone had, in fact, been cooking. Every surface was covered with crumpled tinfoil and scattered flour, chocolate chips and open tin cans, measuring spoons and cups

I didn't even know we owned, and an overturned blender that looked like it had been dragged behind a truck. And there, surrounded by sheets of newly baked chocolate chip cookies, was my brother, Patch.

Patch is probably the most popular and best-looking guy in his group of friends, and he's always disappearing for days at a time and coming back after a bunch of crazy adventures. It's not like he seeks it out—he's just such a cool, easygoing guy that people are always inviting him along to the Hamptons or to parties out in Brooklyn that last entire weekends, and sometimes he just forgets to tell us he's not coming back. So I wasn't exactly sure why he was hanging out in the kitchen scratching out answers to the *New York Times* crossword puzzle. My orange Pomeranian, Noodles, was curled up at his feet, fast asleep.

When Patch noticed me standing in the doorway, no doubt looking completely shell-shocked, he lifted his glass of milk in salute, like some TV sitcom dad, and gave me a cheery grin.

"You guys," I whispered in disbelief, picking a burned cookie off the nearest tray. "What's going on? Did we start getting a subscription to *Good Housekeeping* or something? Or wait, did Mom and Dad do something I'm absolutely going to hate?"

Patch and Feb exchanged significant looks.

"I think we should tell her," said Patch.

Feb pulled a chair out from the table and motioned for me to sit down on it. She sat next to me and took my hands in hers. I felt the grit of baking powder on her palms. "I've got to tell you something, Flanny, but you're not going to like it."

"If it's that you and Patch have been replaced by robots, I'm right there with you," I said with a smirk.

Feb squeezed my hand. "Mom and Dad left this morning for Beijing. They're going to Cambodia and then to Thailand from there, and I'm not sure when they'll be back."

I felt my face crumple. "They said they were going to stick around here for a while. I can't believe they did this again—without even telling me!"

Ever since I was little, my parents have traveled a lot. For a few years before I was in school, we even lived on a sailboat, floating around from port to port, although all I really remember about the experience is the way the tossing of the ocean made me spill my juice. Point is, I'm used to them being gone a lot, and Patch and Feb have sort of half-raised me from the time they were old enough to stay home by themselves. But right after I started high school, Mom and Dad came back from our summerhouse in Connecticut and announced that they were going to keep an eye on me for once. And, even though I know most kids in the world would eat ten boxes of bugs to be in my situation, I was glad to hear they'd be sticking around for a while.

Now it was all starting to make sense: the family dinners we'd eaten at different restaurants around the city the last few nights—the haircut certificate Mom had given me "just for being such a great kid!" They'd been feeling guilty. And now they were gone.

I leaned over and scooped Noodles into my arms. He woke up and started licking my face with his little pink tongue. "But they just got back. Why would they take off again so soon?"

"There's a human rights conference in Beijing with Bon Jovi and Bono and some congressmen, and it was all very last-minute and impromptu, and when the pedal hit the metal they just couldn't say no. Mom told me herself that she wouldn't leave you for the world—except she had to make an exception because right now, the world needs her!"

"Wait, Mom talked to you about this?" Getting information from Feb is like playing telephone with a bunch of fourth-graders after they've eaten peanut butter sandwiches: not very reliable.

"Well, they only found out they were going a couple days ago. And you know how they hate long good-byes."

I shook my head. "I really wanted them to be here for my freshman year."

She and Patch smiled at each other, like they'd been waiting for this.

"That's where we come in," said Patch. "We knew you'd be upset about Mom and Dad being out of town. So we figured we'd give you the next best thing."

"Grandma and Granddad?" I asked, perking up a little.

"No, silly!" Feb swatted at me with her martini glass and spilled gin onto my jeans. "Us!"

"Wait, what do you mean?"

"Feb and I thought we could be like Mom and Dad," Patch explained. "Or actually, more like somebody else's mom and dad. A mom and dad who're around all the time. Feb's learning to cook and she's going to start walking Noodles, and I'm going to get some tools tomorrow to fix the leaky faucet in the bathtub. We're really going to keep an eye out for you this time, Flan. We're taking it seriously."

Even though I was sad my parents had taken off again, I was used to it by now, and I couldn't help but grin at the earnest, worried expressions on my siblings' faces. I saw where this was going, and it was already hilarious. It would be like the year when Patch resolved to stop letting girls fall in love with him—my brother and sister would keep up this *Leave It to Beaver* act for two days, at most, and then forget about it entirely. But for the time being I decided to humor them.

"Okay." Noodles wriggled happily on my lap while I scratched the soft, floofy fur behind his ears. "So what's on the menu tonight? I'm starving."

"Meatloaf!" Feb triumphantly rose out of her chair and walked to the oven. But when she opened the oven door, a tornado of black soot poured out, and for the second time that day I was completely engulfed by acrid-smelling smoke.

About two hours later, after one emergency trip to the grocery store and a second emergency trip to the pharmacy for burn balm and Band-Aids, Feb's meatloaf was finished, and it actually looked pretty amazing. Patch set the table, and I helped carry side dishes over while Feb cut thick slices of the meatloaf. We all sat down and unfolded napkins on our laps. It was just like being in a restaurant or something, except with Noodles prancing around underfoot, waving his paws and begging for table scraps. Sometimes I think he's not a dog at all, just some kind of ultra-cute anime version of a baby fox.

"So, Flan, you never told me how your day went,"

Feb said, spooning mashed potatoes onto her plate.

"There's not much to tell. Nothing too exciting happened. Just classes. I think I bombed a quiz in English." I took a bite of asparagus. It was really pretty tasty, even if it was kind of limp. I swallowed. "What about you two?"

Patch tilted his head to the side, thinking. "Well, Mickey was going to get his bike fixed. But now he's thinking about getting an ATV."

"Wait a second," Feb cut in, staring daggers at me from across the table. "You bombed a quiz?"

I almost choked on my roll. Feb was really getting into this concerned-mom role. "It's really okay. I've been doing fine in that class. I just had to spend some extra time on my bio homework last night, so I didn't really get a chance to study. God, Feb, don't look so worried."

Although I got a little worried myself at that moment. Mentioning biology reminded me of Adam, Meredith, and Judith. Luckily, I had SBB's No Adam Rule in case things got out of control and my friends started obsessing over Adam's every move, like they had done with Tony. Adam definitely wasn't worth the trouble, although it had been nice how he noticed my haircut—Bennett still hadn't figured out what was different about me. . . . I forced myself to push those thoughts away and focus on what Feb was saying.

"Well," said February, "I've been working my butt off with this internship."

"You have an internship?" I tried to picture Feb making copies, typing, even operating a stapler, but somehow the image didn't gel. Then again, if she was going to the grocery store and making meatloaf, anything was possible. "Where is it? When did it start?"

"About four days ago." Feb dabbed at her lips with a napkin, then picked up her martini glass again. "A friend of mine was working at this law firm, but she was moonlighting as a flair bartender and she got hit on the head with a schnapps bottle. So I'm covering for her till she gets back."

"Wow. What law firm is it?"

"Jenkins and Lowe. They mostly do contracts, royalties, stuff like that. Hey, I think they represent Sara-Beth Benny."

"Oh." I made a mental note not to mention that to SBB. She hates her lawyer almost as much as she hates her agent.

We finished eating about twenty minutes later. It had been a really nice dinner—amazingly, nothing was burned, mushy, or raw. Even Noodles seemed to like the scraps I sneaked him under the table. We were enjoying one another's company so much that Patch turned on the stereo and we all listened to this new indie band he'd found and even washed the dishes together instead of just leaving them piled in the sink like usual. Then we started a game of Monopoly, which I hadn't played since I was about eight years old, drank fresh cappuccinos from our espresso maker, and munched on cookies for dessert. My brother and sister can be pretty cool to hang out with, and it was all so pleasant I started to hope I was wrong and that this caring-parents routine might go on for a while. I had just polished off my third cookie and was starting to feel my stomach expand in a way that I couldn't call comfortable when the doorbell rang.

"I'll get it," I volunteered, scooping Noodles up in my arms.

"Be careful," Feb called. "Keep the chain on. It might be a psycho."

I rolled my eyes. But when I opened the door, I dropped Noodles and shrieked.

Chapter 7

Standing there on our front step, holding a bunch of yellow lilies, was Bennett.

"That's so romantic!" I gave him a big hug. "Lilies are my favorite. What're you doing here?"

Bennett handed me the bouquet, then bent down to pet Noodles, who was jumping up on his legs. "I was just at a record store on Bleecker, and I thought I'd come by to see if you felt like getting some ice cream."

"Come on in—you can finally meet Feb! We were all just playing Monopoly." I held the door open for him.

"Monopoly?" Bennett echoed, following me inside. He glanced around and seemed about as surprised as I'd been by how clean it was. The last few times he'd been over, the living room had been covered with pizza boxes and empty cans my brother's friends had abandoned. I led him into the living room and introduced to him Feb.

When Bennett offered his hand for my sister to shake, she took it cordially, and—if I read her right—a bit suspiciously.

"Isn't it a little late to just be 'dropping by'?" she asked with an arched eyebrow. I elbowed her in the side.

Bennett shifted his feet and smiled nervously. "I promise to have her back soon. Can we bring you guys any ice cream?"

"No, we just had cookies." Feb crossed her arms and gave me a sharp look. "Just don't stay out too late. It's a school night."

"All right . . . *Mom*." I grabbed Bennett's hand and pulled him out the door, wondering if I'd spoken too soon about liking this superparents routine. Outside, we kept holding hands as we walked along the sidewalk.

"That was weird," he said. "Your sister seemed so . . . Well, from what you said, I had pictured her as some sort of party goddess, but she was kind of acting like Barbara Bush. Only meaner."

"Oh, Feb's nuts and totally unpredictable. She'll drop the Stepford act when she gets bored of it—which I'm guessing will be in about two days." I laughed.

"Minus the third degree back there, it's actually kind of cute. She even baked cookies."

Bennett looked at me almost shyly out of the corner of his eye, "I hope you saved room for ice cream."

"I always do." I smiled. Like Judith and Meredith, he'd been a little intimidated by my crazy family and famous friends at first, but now that he was getting to know everybody, it seemed like he was fitting in just fine. And I knew that once Feb was back to normal she'd like him a lot, too.

We walked down my block, stopping for a minute at the art gallery on my street, which had a bunch of cool brass sculptures in the window. Some of them had moving parts—like big sideways propellers—and Bennett said they reminded him of the Alexander Calder mobiles he'd seen on an art field trip to the Whitney Museum, which made me squeeze his hand even tighter. He's such a smart guy.

"I really like this neighborhood," he said as we turned onto West Fourth Street. A bunch of New York University students were hanging out and drinking coffee at the Bean Garden and at the Starbucks across the street. "There's always so much going on. Up on the West Side, I feel like there's nothing but Citibanks and grocery stores and people my parents' age—the whole place closes down at eight P.M."

"But I like your neighborhood too." Bennett lives up near Riverside Park, and when he had a party there earlier in the semester, I thought his building was beautiful. It looked like a big white cake. All the buildings in my neighborhood are small and kind of old. When I was a kid, Greenwich Village used to remind me of the town in Pinocchio: all the streets are crooked and narrow.

"Well, I guess the grass is always greener, right?" Bennett kissed me on the forehead. "Maybe I just like coming down here because I get to hang out with you."

My heart melted as we walked along Bleecker Street, passing Cynthia Rowley and Intermix, and all the other little boutiques where they kind of know me. We passed a record store and Bennett stopped to look in the window.

"Have I ever played you those old Velvet Underground records of my dad's?" he asked. "They're kind of collectors' items, but he lets me borrow them. We should listen to them the next time you're at my apartment."

"Sure. They sound really cool." We kept walking and crossed Seventh Avenue. We had wanted to go to Cones, but when we got there the line went out the door, so we headed to Mary's Dairy on West Fourth

Street instead. I love ice cream—it's pretty much my favorite food in the world—and that place is one of my favorites because of all the wacky flavors they have, like cappuccino Kahlùa, pumpkin, Damson plum sorbet, vanilla Swiss almond, and, my all time personal favorite, hazelnut fudge. That particular night, though, I ordered cinnamon pecan with mini raspberry chocolate truffles. Bennett thought it sounded gross, but it looked delicious to me. He ordered plain vanilla, as usual. There wasn't really anyplace to sit down—Mary's Dairy is sort of small, with only a few little round tables, and NYU students had invaded here, too—so we decided to eat our ice cream outside. Bennett insisted on paying for every-thing, and even held the door for me on the way out.

"Hey, I was wondering if we could go to the comic book store," he said as we walked out down the side-walk, carrying our cups of ice cream. "Jules was in there the other day, and they have a copy of this old *Green Lantern* issue from the seventies that I want to check out."

"Sure." I said, but truthfully my heart sank a little. Superheroes are cool and everything, but I'd been to comic book stores with Bennett in the past, and I knew that once he found something he was interested in, he'd just stand there and read it cover to cover—

or, worse, start discussing it with the equally obsessed guy working behind the counter. They'd get into some argument about a minor detail and have to dig through a million old issues to find out who was right. "Or I can just wait outside for a second while you run in and get it." A cab pulled to a stop next to us, and a man wearing a Burberry overcoat and carrying peach-colored tulips rushed into August, the French bistro on the corner.

"Oh, no, there's no way I can buy it. These old ones go for like a hundred bucks apiece. I just want to flip through it in the store. You'll probably find it really interesting—in the seventies, the series started to get socially relevant and kind of edgy."

Bennett droned on about the *Green Lantern* series, explaining the various plotlines, but my mind started to wander almost immediately. I can never really keep all those characters straight in my head. They all sort of look the same in their masks and tights and capes. And for some reason, all of Bennett's talk about the Green Lantern got me thinking about the color green and a certain quarterback with chartreuse-green eyes. . . . I checked my watch. It was almost nine, and I wanted to get home to finish up my bio worksheets in case Adam needed help with them tomorrow in class. Whoa. Back up, Flan. Why was I thinking about Adam when I was out on a date with Bennett? Before I had time to figure it out, Bennett forced me back to reality with a short tug on the ends of my hair.

I blinked. "What was that for?"

"I finally know why you look different!" He grinned as he threw his arm around my shoulders, clearly proud of himself. "Just now. You have bangs and your hair's kind of . . . fringier or something."

"You got it." I'd been wanting Bennett to notice, but now that he had, I actually felt kind of sad.

"Ha. I knew I'd figure it out eventually." Bennett stopped walking and guided me across the street to a store front displaying brightly colored comic books and a cardboard cutout of Captain America with RIP written on a paper sign around his neck. "Damn!" he muttered.

"What? Captain America died?"

"Well, that too. But . . ." He pointed to another, much smaller, sign in the window: ON VACATION. KEVIN'S WORLD OF COMICS WILL RESUME NORMAL HOURS FRIDAY. Unbidden, I thought of Adam reading ahead in the English textbook, and a little part of me wondered why Bennett was only interested in books about radioactive spiders and disfigured villains who take over the world.

"Oh, darn."

Bennett shook his head. "Well, I guess we'll just have to come back later, then."

I paused. "Um, right." At least that gave me a couple more days to think up an excuse. Like maybe I'd be recovering from a radioactive spider bite.

Chapter 8

*A*fter school on Tuesday, Meredith, Judith, and I decided to walk over to the Soda Shop to do homework and have a milk shake. I'd just taken a history unit test, and I was exhausted. The Mesopotamians were probably an interesting group of people back in the day, but trying to remember all that stuff about law codes and bas-reliefs was starting to give me a headache. I was really looking forward to spending a little time chilling out with my friends, which seemed in the realm of possibility because Judith and Meredith appeared to be getting along again. I hadn't even had to set the No Adam Rule, because, somewhat miraculously, neither of them had mentioned him since the pep rally.

We all met up at Judith's locker, then rode the escalator down together, laughing and joking about our classes that day. Apparently, Meredith's art history teacher had cued up the wrong slides on the PowerPoint projector, so they'd spent half their class looking at pictures of her Hawaiian vacation instead of the Italian Renaissance paintings they were supposed to be studying.

We were pushing through the double doors on the first floor, laughing at Meredith's descriptions of Mrs. Billing's grass skirt, when someone jostled past us. I wasn't really paying attention, but Meredith and Judith both stopped in their tracks, mouths agape. It was Adam. He stopped and grinned at us in that friendly way of his.

"Sorry," he said. "I didn't see you guys there."

"It's all right," Judith managed weakly, looking like she was about to have a heart attack.

"Well, I've got to head to practice." He raised the water bottle he had in his left hand, as if making a toast. "I'll catch you later."

"Yeah," Meredith whispered. "See you in class tomorrow."

He took off, but my two friends didn't move. They just stood there, staring, until he went up the escalator and disappeared. Finally I couldn't take the silence anymore.

"Wow, you'd think he went to heaven. What about us? Are we still going to the Soda Shop?" I asked. No response. "Hello? Guys? Earth to Judith and Meredith!" I snapped my fingers.

"Did you see that?" Judith breathed. "Did you see what just happened?"

"Yes!" Meredith's voice was full of wonder, and her eyes sparkled. "I can't believe it."

I glanced in the direction of the escalator, then back toward the two of them. "What do you mean?"

"Adam likes me," they both said at the same time.

And just like that, the Adam spell was cast again. They blinked, then spun to look at each other angrily.

"What are you talking about?" Judith demanded. "He looked right at me!"

"He told me he'd catch me later!" Meredith furrowed her brow. "Didn't you hear him? He said, 'I'll catch you later.' And I said, 'Yes, in English class.' And then he smiled—partly because he loves reading poetry, but mostly because he can't wait to see me again."

"You're completely delusional!" Judith exploded. "He said, 'Catch you later,' to all of us! You're just reading into everything because your imagination is out of control!"

"Well, then maybe he was *looking* at all of us too! And you just think he was looking at you because you always have to win at everything!"

"What is wrong with you two?" I yelled over them. All around us, clusters of happy Stuy students shouted friendly good-byes to one other, while here my friends were just plain shouting at each other. What would I do if Meredith and Judith and I weren't friends anymore? The school would be such a big, lonely place without them.

I grabbed their hands and pulled them outside. They followed me as I turned and started walking in the direction of the Soda Shop. "Have you two lost your minds? This is ridiculous. You've been best friends for years . . . and you've barely known Adam for a month."

Taxis and buses rattled along Chambers Street, and a stretch Hummer pulled up to the curb next to us, its mirrored windows reflecting the image of three very crabby looking girls.

"There's a lot more to it than that," said Meredith, switching her sage green woven purse to her left shoulder. "Between me and Adam, I mean. I really think he likes me. He talks to me in English practically all the time, and we have so much in common. The other day he asked me for a pencil, and you know artistic people prefer pencils to ballpoints, right? He might have even been using it to write poems for me during class."

I cringed a little at this confession, but Judith did something way meaner. She laughed out loud.

"You're crazy. Did it ever occur to you that he probably just needed a pencil?" Judith demanded, flipping her blond hair over her shoulder.

"Oh yeah?" Meredith stopped short in front of Yoga Connection, whose exercise rooms, according to Feb, are as hot as Death Valley. Through the window a whole class full of women were sweating and bending themselves into pretzel-like shapes. While I couldn't totally see the appeal, I wished I were in there sweating like crazy instead of listening to my friends fight about Adam.

"Well, if I'm so crazy," Meredith challenged, "then why do you think he likes you so much? Did he propose to you or something? Send you flowers?"

"No." Judith smiled proudly. "But he did tell me the weather's been great for football lately."

"What's that supposed to mean?" Meredith asked.

"That he wants me to come to his game on Saturday, obviously." She stared at us meaningfully. Meredith looked at me, and I shrugged. "Because he has a secret crush on me," Judith explained. She brushed her hands together like the case was closed.

Meredith and I didn't say anything for a long time. Somewhere in the distance, a siren howled. Two pigeons cooed on a windowsill high above our heads. Finally, I spoke. If there was ever going to be a perfect moment to bring up SBB's idea, it was now.

"Listen, I've got a suggestion, okay? Since both of you like Adam, but neither of you really knows him that well yet—"

"Hey!" both my friends exclaimed in unison. I held up one finger.

"I said yet. Anyway, how about you just agree to an official No Adam Rule, where neither of you go after him? That way you'll know neither of you will be flirting with him, so you can stop fighting about it. Maybe you'll even meet some other cute guys who you like just as much." I smiled hopefully.

Meredith and Judith stared at me like I'd just suggested they play ukuleles while wearing swimsuits made of clamshells and seaweed at Stuy's next pep rally.

"Um, thanks for the advice, Flan," Judith said, a little snarkily, "but I think we can work this out ourselves. No offense, but it's not really any of your business."

That kind of made me mad, but I tried not to show it. "How can you say it's not my business? I care about you guys. If you're acting like you're about to kill each other, it's obviously going to bother me." I stared down at the sidewalk. Someone had drawn a heart in the concrete when it was still wet. I traced its curve with my toe. "If you really want to duke it out over this guy, be my guest. I just think it's a shame, you know?"

Meredith looked down, like she felt bad about it, and Judith didn't look too happy either. I knew I was making them feel guilty, but what else could I say? It was true.

"I guess that's fair," Meredith said in a little voice. "Since we can't both have him, then neither of us should get to."

Judith eyed her suspiciously for a moment, then seemed to relax. She stuck out her pinky finger. "No Adam Rule?"

"No Adam Rule," Meredith agreed, looping her little finger around Judith's and shaking it.

"Yay!" I threw my arms around both of them. "Now can we go to the Soda Shop? I'm dying for a strawberry malt."

I took out my cell phone as we started walking again and flipped it open. Eleven missed calls. I scrolled to my missed-calls list, my heart beating quickly. Two calls was one thing but *eleven*? And all from . . . *Feb*? I pressed the SEND button and waited while it rang. We were just at the Soda Shop but I stopped before going in.

"Hang on a sec," I said. The Soda Shop really is one of the cutest little places in New York and I was kind of excited to be going in. It looks just like something out of one of those old Norman Rockwell paintings: it has gum-ball jars, a marble counter, and even an old-fashioned soda fountain. Going there is like stepping back to a time where all the girls wore ponytails and saddle shoes. . . .

"Hey, what's going on?" I asked Feb as a dog walker with a herd of Dalmatians and Chows passed us. "Is everything okay?"

"Flan, where are you?"

"I'm going to the Soda Shop with Meredith and Judith. Why?"

"You're hanging out with friends again? And on a school afternoon? You know, I think it was pretty nice of me to let you go out last night with Bennett, even though you failed your English quiz. But I think you should come home right now and study. I don't want your grades to drop. Besides, it's getting late."

I looked at my watch. It was only 4:03.

"Excuse me—you 'let' me go out? You've got to be kidding me, Feb. Besides, I'm going to work on stuff there."

"I really don't think that's a good idea." Feb paused, and I could hear pots clattering, water running in the sink, and Noodles yapping his head off on the other end of the line. "I want you home where it's quiet. Maybe I can even help you with your English if you're having trouble."

"But Feb," I protested, exasperatedly, "English is barely your first language—"

"No back talk! I mean it, Flan. I'm getting dinner ready now, and I expect you home in thirty minutes." She hung up.

Meredith and Judith looked at me curiously as I snapped my phone shut angrily and shoved it back into my teal Luella Bartley purse. It was one thing for Feb to make dinner and ask me about my day—that was actually kind of nice—but what right did she have to boss me around and tell me that I couldn't hang out with my friends after school? She could buy all the aprons she wanted, but that didn't actually make her my mother.

On the other hand, though, all the fighting between Meredith and Judith hadn't exactly put me in the mood for an extended afternoon with them—even if the NAR was in effect.

"Listen, guys, I'm really sorry, but apparently Feb needs me at home," I said, rolling my eyes. "But thanks again for agreeing to the No Adam Rule. You're sure everything's okay with you guys now?"

"Of course." Judith adjusted the strap of her navy blue French Connection tank and flipped her hair over her shoulder.

"Yeah, and thanks for all your advice, Flan. I think it will really help," Meredith added. "We'll see you tomorrow morning."

I stepped back and looked at them. They looked at me with innocent smiles on their faces as they linked arms.

"Want to take the subway uptown?" Meredith asked Judith.

"Sounds like a plan," Judith replied with a nod.

"All right . . . 'bye, then," I told them as I turned to leave.

But when I looked back, they had already dropped each other's arms.

I woke up the next morning with a huge knot in my stomach. I wondered at first if it was just the after-effects of the somewhat unappetizing version of cheese soufflé Feb had served for dinner the night before. But as I put on my charcoal gray Miu Miu blazer with the colorful polka-dotted lining, I realized it wasn't the cheese that was making me feel like I had a miniature Noodles rolling around in my stomach. It was my quarterback-loving friends.

I was so worried and distracted that on my walk to school I tripped over the leash of a shih tzu on the corner of Spring and Varick Streets, and then almost walked out in front of an M20 bus speeding down-town. Once I got to school, another thing added to my stress about Judith and Meredith: the source of dis-cord himself, Adam. Suddenly it seemed like he was popping up everywhere: near the third-floor drinking fountain, in the cafeteria, by the fifth-floor escalator. It wasn't like I thought he was following me—that would have been pretty conceited—but then I began to get a little worried that *he* might think *I* was following him. Which I wasn't, obviously. But just in case, I started trying to avoid him, which of course didn't work, because I didn't know which way he'd be walking, and after English, I took an ill-fated detour around the gym only to practically knock him over by the second-floor bathrooms and drop all my books like a royal klutz.

"Oh, wow, I'm so sorry!" I could feel my face turning red as he rubbed his arm where I'd bumped into him.

"Don't worry about it." He picked up my geometry textbook and handed it to me. He was wearing a plain gray fitted T-shirt, and I noticed that his hair was a little mussed, like he'd forgotten to comb it or something. "You know, we need a new defensive lineman for the team. You interested?"

"Thanks, but no," I said, grabbing the book from him. "I'll see you in bio, I guess."

I quickly scurried off around the corner, feeling both embarrassed and irrationally annoyed. It was like he knew about the No Adam Rule and was secretly trying to thwart it at every turn. As glad as I was not to be at Mallard Day anymore, I realized my life had been a little less complicated when there were no boys around.

I did manage to shake a little bit of Adam-water out of my ears during math class, though. I concentrated on isosceles triangles instead of *love* triangles, and on Bennett and the bouquet of lemon yellow lilies he'd given me instead of the flowery way Meredith and Judith talked about Adam. But bio was right after math, and I knew that there would be no escaping Adam and his comfy-sweater-sea-green eyes there.

Apparently there would be no escaping my Adam-obsessed friends, either, because waiting right outside my biology class was a freshly lip-glossed Judith.

"Flan! There you are!" she exclaimed, rushing over to hug me like it had been years, rather than hours, since we'd last seen each other. When she let go, she craned her neck to look past me into the classroom.

I shifted my schoolbag on my arm. "Judith, isn't your history class on the fourth floor? Won't you be late?"

"Uh, yeah," she said absently, her eyes darting around, doubtlessly searching for a certain football player. Her eyes shifted to a spot two inches above my left shoulder as she reached into her green leather briefcase and pulled out a chewed-up Bic pen. "I forgot to give this back to you after I borrowed it three weeks ago. I thought you might need it for your lab."

"Thanks . . . I guess." I gingerly took the mangled pen from her. "Well, I have to head inside. You should probably get going too."

Judith nodded, looking as though she wished she could followed me into bio. She stood there as I walked through the door, and then she leaned so far over the threshold to wave good-bye that for a moment I thought she might actually fall into the classroom.

When she finally left, I tossed the pen into the garbage and shook my head. Adam and his friends were sitting in the back, so I slid into a desk in the front row, as far away from them as possible, and didn't look up from my notebook until after class had started. Our teacher, Mr. Phelps, announced we were doing a new project—it was time to grow baby frogs from tadpoles and observe them at all stages of life. It was going to take more than a month, and our final logbooks would be worth a third of our grade. And because my life wasn't complicated enough already, Mr. Phelps thought it would be super fun to assign us new lab partners and pair me with—yep, you guessed it—Adam.

Lucky me.

I worked on keeping my face expressionless as Adam and I walked to our new lab table in the back of the room. I noticed that he'd combed his hair since I last saw him, and at that moment I decided to also place myself under the No Adam Rule, but in a No Being Friends with Adam way. I would do everything in my power to keep our conversation professional—frogs, bio, that was it. Judith's using the gross pen as an excuse to see Adam reinforced just how much she and Meredith needed to stick to the No Adam Rule. And I couldn't exactly ask them to keep away from Adam only to become friends with him myself, right?

"Hey—I never asked how your English quiz went," Adam said as he sat down on one of the circular metal stools at our station.

"It went okay, I think." I didn't want to be totally rude, so I gave him a tight smile. "Thanks again for taking me through that ending."

"No problem." He put his elbow a couple inches away from mine on the black Formica tabletop. "I love a good story."

I dropped my arm into my lap. What was the matter with him? I cleared my throat and made myself sound as no-nonsense and scientific as possible.

"So, frogs. *Rana catesbeiana*," I said briskly.

"Rana cat-a-what?" Adam's lips curved into a

smile as he gave me a confused look from across the counter.

"*Rana catesbeiana*." I tapped a page in our textbook. "That's the scientific name for the American bullfrog."

Adam nodded slowly, staring at me like I was crazy. Which was probably a good thing in terms of the NAR, especially if it scared him off a little.

I was thankful when Mr. Phelps came over and placed a jar filled with dirty water on our table. Inside, a little tadpole was squirming around, flipping its tails and bumping its head against the glass.

"Look at that." Adam leaned forward to examine the tadpole as Mr. Phelps moved onto the table behind us. "Our boy. What should we name him? Kermit?"

"Too obvious." I picked up the jar and squinted at the little guy. He was slimy but cute, with big buggy eyes and the stumpy beginnings of back legs. "Why don't we call him Bogie?"

"As in Humphrey Bogart? That's great. I love old movies."

"You do?" I stared at Adam in surprise. I love old movies almost as much as I love ice cream.

"Of course. I loved Bogie in *The Petrified Forest*. You ever see that one?"

I set Bogie the tadpole's jar back on the counter. "That's so weird, I seriously just rented that this past weekend!" What is it about guys liking old movies that makes them seem really sophisticated?

Adam smiled and locked eyes with me, and that was when I started to get a little nervous. Who *was* this guy?

"Remember to wear your rubber gloves and lab goggles while working with the specimens," Mr. Phelps reminded the class as he handed out shakers of frog food. "Try to take as many notes on the frogs' behavior as possible. You will be graded on the volume and accuracy of your data."

I took my lab goggles out of my schoolbag and grimaced. "Ugh. I hate these things."

"Yeah, they do kind of fog up." Adam reached into his schoolbag as well.

"That, and they look stupid. On me, anyway—like I'm a big bug."

Adam put his on right away and looked over at me. With his square jaw and curly hair, the goggles didn't look too bad. "Let me see."

I sighed and stretched my goggles over my head. The elastic band made the back of my hair stick up. Adam laughed.

"No, they're cute!"

"Cute like Bogie, maybe." The goggles felt a little too tight, so I took them off to adjust the strap.

Just then Adam reached across the table. Before I had a chance to react, he lightly touched my forehead. "Oh no—you already have goggle lines."

I took a small step backward and pulled on my gloves. "Bogie looks kind of hungry. Maybe we should feed him." My forehead tingled a little where he'd touched me.

Adam unscrewed the tadpole jar and tapped a few flakes of frog food out onto the surface of the water. Bogie ate them up super fast, flicking with his tongue just like a regular-size frog. It was incredibly cute and funny, and I couldn't help but laugh along with Adam.

"It says here he'll start developing lungs in two weeks," Adam read from one of the photographs Mr. Phelps had passed out. "They sure grow up fast, don't they?"

"Pretty soon we'll be helping him with college applications," I agreed.

Adam started filling in one of the charts. "Nah, he's going to take after me and do the dumb-jock thing. He'll get a scholarship to some football factory if he's lucky."

"Don't be ridiculous. You're a smart guy," I said,

surprising myself by actually meaning it. Between reading ahead in English and liking old movies, Adam seemed to have a lot of interests.

"I don't know." He sighed. "Most people see the jersey and assume all I'm good at is throwing a ball around and tackling people."

I frowned. Hadn't I said that about Adam when Meredith told me she liked him? It had been pretty judgmental of me, and I'd clearly been wrong. "I think you guys must work harder than most people realize, since you have to go to practice and get all your work done on time."

"It is kind of a lot. And to be honest, I'm a little nervous for our first game this Saturday." Adam glanced over at me. "Any chance you'll be there?"

"Oh, I don't know . . ." I faltered, imaging Meredith and Judith's wounded expressions if they knew Adam had asked whether I going to be at the game, even though he was probably just being friendly. Invoking the No Adam Rule, I said, "Football's not really my thing." Not wanting to look at him, I tapped Bogie's jar and watched as he swam right up to the glass to stare out at me with his googly eyes.

But Adam went on, undaunted. "Well, Brooklyn Tech's supposed to be one of the better teams in the conference this year, so it should be a good matchup.

You should definitely check it out. You might surprise yourself by liking it." Adam held my eyes for a second as he handed the worksheet back to me. "And it'd mean a lot to see you there."

The bell rang and all around us kids started slamming their books shut and putting their papers into their folders. I quickly grabbed my schoolbag and started throwing things inside. Adam hoisted his backpack onto his shoulders and looked at me expectantly.

I rubbed my forehead, struggling with how to answer. Noncommittal seemed the best route. "We're supposed to wear school colors, right?"

He grinned. "Red and blue. I'll keep an eye out for you."

I heaved a huge sigh as I finished gathering my things and stuck Bogie on a back shelf with the other tadpoles. This bio unit seemed like it could be fun, but I gave myself an F in abiding by the No Adam Rule.

Chapter 10

After school, I found Bennett by my locker, looking adorable as usual. He was leaning against the wall, wearing a plaid Dickies shirt and a brown corduroy jacket. His dirty blond hair fell into his eyes as he thumbed through an old comic, and his mouth was set into a funny little frown of concentration that made him look smart and a little bit silly at the same time. But as soon as he saw me out of the corner of his eye, he looked up and gave me the sweetest, nicest smile—like there was no one in the world he'd rather see. I found myself beaming right back. Okay, so yes, Adam was totally hot, but Bennett, with his chipped tooth and eager blue eyes, was totally *adorable*.

"Hey," he said, shoving off the wall with his left foot. "Just thought I'd stop by and see if you wanted to go to the Bean Garden for a latte."

"I wish I could, but Feb's been acting like a

cartoon version of somebody's mother. She wants me to come home right after school now." I sighed. "Pretty soon she'll be putting bars on my windows."

"Or maybe she'll hire a bouncer to keep me out of your house—isn't that more her style?"

I laughed. "At this point, I can almost imagine her doing that."

"Anything I can do to help?" Bennett asked me as I twisted the dial on my locker door.

I put the books and papers I needed in my bag and slammed the metal door shut. "Yes, on second thought, you can take me out for coffee." Bennett was so sweet and thoughtful. I grabbed his hand and gave it a friendly squeeze. "I haven't gotten a chance to talk to you all day."

"So, I'm thinking about sending some of my clips from the *Spectator* to this writing contest," said Bennett, as we walked down the second-floor hallway. "It's sort of a long shot, but the person they choose gets to write a weekly column for teens on the *Time Out New York* Web site."

"Wow, Bennett, that's so exciting." We reached the end of the hallway, but when we turned the corner into the stairwell, I almost gasped out loud. There, coming down the stairs from the third floor, was Adam McGregor.

For some reason, running into him when I was with Bennett made me feel slightly panicky. But Adam didn't seem fazed at all to see me with another guy. He just smiled, and it occurred to me that maybe I'd misunderstood the way he'd acted in bio and at lunch. He seemed to be friendly with everyone, and the fact that he'd been so nice to me probably didn't mean anything except that he was a nice guy. *Whoa.* I'd been acting just like Meredith and Judith—reading way too much into totally innocent conversations. The idea should have cheered me up—one less thing to worry about!—but for some reason it didn't comfort me quite as much as it should have.

"Hey, Flan," he said with an easy grin. "How's it going?"

"Oh, hey, Adam." I said, trying to sound as nonchalant as he did. "Have you met Bennett?"

Adam kept smiling, but I could have sworn that a flicker of something—disappointment, maybe?—came across his face. Almost immediately, though, he turned to Bennett and offered his hand for him to shake.

Bennett took his hand, glancing between Adam and me. "Nice to meet you. So . . . you're in bio together, right?

"Lab partners—we have a tadpole together." Adam

gave me a playful wink, and I blushed a little. Then he pointed to the comic book Bennett still had in his hand. "Hey—is that *Green Lantern*?"

"Yep—number seventy-five," Bennett said, holding up the cover for Adam to see.

Adam took the comic book from Bennett and flipped through the thin pages. "My brother's obsessed with *Green Lantern*. He has a bunch of these comics—all the way back to the beginning of the series."

"Really?" Bennett lit up, and if I didn't know better, I would say he looked at Adam with almost as much adoration as Meredith and Judith had at the pep rally. "You're kidding me. This series is incredible. I only really got into it a few months ago, but the art, the stories—"

"Yeah, that's what Darren always says. He's kind of a nut about it and keeps them locked in a filing cabinet." A girl with curly brown hair squeezed past us to go upstairs, shooting Adam a flirtatious grin in the process. Adam smiled back, and then continued talking to Bennett. "You should come over sometime. He loves showing them off, so I bet he'd be happy to let you check them out."

"That's really nice, Adam," I said, almost to remind them that I was still there. It was kind of weird how they were both totally ignoring me all of a sudden.

"Anyway, Bennett and I were going to go grab a cup of coffee, so we better get going. . . ."

"You want to come with us?" Bennett asked as I started inching toward the stairs. "We're heading down to the Bean Garden."

"I wish I could, but I promised a friend I'd help him with his English homework. If his grades drop any lower, Coach'll have to put him on academic probation."

Bennett looked impressed. "No offense or anything, but I didn't actually think football players helped each other study."

Adam shrugged. "Well, he's one of our best players— it'd hurt to lose him for even a couple games."

"Still, it's cool of you to help him," I agreed, a little grudgingly.

"We'll see how much progress we make. I'm still trying to convince him that *The Catcher in the Rye* isn't about a baseball player." He hefted his backpack down off his shoulder and took out a notebook. "Anyhow, here's my e-mail address. I should be around this weekend if you want to stop by."

"Cool!" Bennett said excitedly. "I'll give you mine, too."

Even though Adam had been nothing but nice to me, it seemed like every time I saw him my life got more complicated. What was this guy's deal, anyway? Tutoring his friends, charming mine . . . and now he was going to hang out with Bennett? As the two of them scribbled down their e-mail addresses, I tried to convince myself that things would be better now that all of us were becoming friends . . . and that being friends with Adam wasn't exactly against the Rule. But I couldn't help feel worried. What if they got together and talked about *me*? I mentally scrolled through all my past conversations with Adam, making sure I hadn't said anything that could possibly be construed as flirtatious.

A second later Adam said good-bye and bounded down the second-floor hallway. Bennett was standing still, looking more than a little awestruck.

"That guy's awesome. And can you believe his brother's a *Green Lantern* fan?"

"I can barely wrap my mind around it," I said dryly. But what I really couldn't wrap my mind around was how easy it was for Adam to charm everybody I knew . . . including me.

Chapter 11

$\mathcal{I}$ had such a nice time with Bennett at coffee that I completely lost track of time. It was dark when I finally got home, and I fumbled with the lock to let myself into the house. Noodles jumped on me the minute I was inside, his dark brown eyes glowing with excitement and love. I sat down on the floor and he kissed my face, wriggling his whole puffball body with happiness. But judging by the awful silence that filled the house, he was the only one glad to see me.

"Hello?" I called. "Anybody home?"

Maybe I'd gotten lucky—maybe Feb and Patch had forgotten about being responsible and taken off for a party at Butter or something. But then a stern voice called, "We're in here, Flan." My good mood deflated instantly, and a searing feeling of annoyance replaced it.

I went into the kitchen, where they were sitting much as they had been the other night, Patch with the

90

newspaper in front of him, Feb dressed in another vintage housewife outfit—gingham dress, white ruffly apron—with a pair of knitting needles and a ball of yarn in her lap. This time, though, there weren't any trays of cookies on the table, and Feb and Patch were both looking at me with deadly serious expressions.

"What?" I said, setting down my bag and purse. "Stop with the silent treatment already." I walked over to the fridge to get myself a bottle of juice.

"Hey, Flanny, take a seat. Feb's pretty worked up," said Patch.

I snorted as I popped open a Nantucket Nectar. "Okay, but you guys better make it fast, because I've got a lot of homework."

"Enough with the attitude, Flan," February snapped. "Now listen. The last time Mom and Dad were home, Patch and I saw how happy you were, and we started talking about how maybe a little bit of discipline was just what you needed. Neither of us had that when we were teenagers, and look how we ended up."

I looked from Feb, in her heels and apron, to Patch, who was wearing his usual T-shirt and jeans.

"Yeah, you guys are completely out of control," I said dryly. "And Patch is still a teenager, in case you forgot."

"Listen, Flan, I know this might not make sense to

you now. But at my internship, I'm starting to see the way the real world works, and believe me, it's nothing like the way we grew up. No all-night parties in the middle of the week, no VIP passes, no celebrities. Well, okay, this firm does handle a lot of entertainment cases, but you know what I mean." She wagged her knitting needle at me menacingly. "I hoped it wouldn't come to this, but it's already eight o'clock—you didn't call to tell me where you were, even though I told you yesterday I want you to come straight home after school. So your brother and I"—Patch shifted uncomfortably in his chair—"decided it might help us provide you with structure if we set some ground rules."

I laughed so hard, strawberry-guava juice almost came shooting out my nose. "You're going to give me *rules*? I'm the good one, remember?"

Feb picked up a piece of paper from the table. A recipe for mojitos was scribbled on the back.

"Rule number one," she read. "Come home directly after school. Do not pass go, do not collect two hundred dollars."

"What?" I exploded. "That's totally ridiculous. When am I supposed to hang out with my friends? And hello? Are you familiar with the word *hypocrisy*?"

"Friends are more than welcome here. If they're not the sort of people you're willing to bring into this house, well . . . then maybe they're not friends worth having." Feb looked down at her piece of paper again. "Rule number two. You now have an eleven o'clock curfew."

"Curfew?"

"Rule number three. Leave your bedroom door open when you have boys over."

"Sometimes when Bennett and I are studying, Patch is down here playing the Clash so loud the walls shake! We shut the door for quiet."

"Rule number four. No clubbing until you're twenty-one."

This was beyond ridiculous—it was totally unfair. All these years, I'd put up with Patch's wild parties and February disappearing for weeks at a time. Now I was supposed to follow their rules? No freakin' way.

"Okay, I've had it." I slammed my juice bottle down on the tabletop and stood up. "Feb, you only turned twenty-one three weeks ago, and you've been a fixture in the New York club scene for years. Patch is only eighteen and the bartenders at Lotus know his name. You guys are really being totally awful and you know it."

I picked up my quilted Marc Jacobs bag and stormed upstairs, ignoring the threats to ground me that Feb was yelling at my back.

$\mathscr{I}$ immediately went out on my balcony, and called Sara-Beth Benny to commiserate.

While I waited for her to pick up, I settled down on my bamboo lawn chair and stared up at the sky. My balcony is probably my favorite thing about my bedroom. It's small, but it has a nice view of our yard and the yards of the other town houses, including SBB's. There's a little wrought-iron railing around the edge of it, with flower boxes where I grow mint and rosemary, and just this past weekend, I'd carved a jack-o'-lantern and stuck it out here too.

"Flan?" SBB finally answered on the seventh ring. She sounded out of breath. "Oh my God, I'm so glad it's you."

"Why? What's going on?" I leaned over to light the cinnamon candle inside my pumpkin. It smelled delicious.

"It's a nightmare, is what it is! So I fired Nada and it was a terrible scene—she was crying and yelling gypsy curses and it was drama, drama, drama, and you know my nerves, so I had no choice but to call the police, and of course with all the sirens and me outside in a kimono at ten in the morning, all these horrible, horrible reporters started swarming down the block, and they were snapping pictures and laughing and it was such a terrible scene, I don't think I'll ever recover. So by then I just wanted complete simplicity, just something nice and clean and simple, you know, no more of this embroidery and crystals and giant bronze elephants in every room, because honestly, I just don't need that kind of thing in my life. So I hired a new designer, this Leif Gaardner, and he promised me that he could make me a new living space that would be calm, you know, utterly calm and sterile, and out of all recycled materials, too, if you can believe that—he's done some wonderful things with truck tires in Northern California—and the long and short of it is, I can't stay on the phone because they're delivering it any min— Oh, here they are now! Wait, wait, I've got to go up to my roof!"

"Your roof? Wait, Sara-Beth, what are they delivering?" I stood up and looked over at her house. An enormous hydraulic crane had rumbled to a stop on

Perry Street. A white Tylenol capsule the size of a VW Bug dangled from its jaws.

The portico door to Sara-Beth's roof was flung open and she came running out, waving her spindly arms around frantically. She yelled directions to the crane operator while the capsule ominously swung back and forth from wires that, from where I sitting, didn't look particularly secure.

"Sara-Beth?" I yelled into the phone. I saw her lift her cell phone back up to her ear.

"So, the thing is," SBB shouted, "Leif thinks the problem is wasted space. I'm only one person—how can I be expected to use a whole town house?" She turned toward the crane, flapping her arms and shrieking, "To the right! No, the other right!" To me, she continued, "There's just so much pressure to make use of the living room and the dining room and the ice dispenser and the Jacuzzi, and obviously it's stressing me out. But this pod provides everything I need—nutrition cubes, solar power, even moist cloths for bathing! And the best part is, no wasted space. I won't even be able to turn around in there. It's like a padded cell."

"But Sara-Beth, doesn't living in the pod make your whole town house wasted space?" I frowned at the pod, which looked like it might crash-land at any second.

"What? I can't hear you!" she screamed over the grinding of the crane's machinery.

"Sara-Beth, you love your town house! If you live in the pod, you won't be using any of it."

Sara-Beth didn't answer. The pod was dipping low, right above her bedroom skylight. "No, no, not here! I want it over there!" The pod continued to descend—four little feet, like the claws on the bottom of an old-fashioned bathtub, grazed the top of her house, settling in for a landing, but SBB looked like she was about to cry. "Not here, I said!" Suddenly, she let out an anguished shriek and began beating the sides of the pod with her tiny, angry fists. Even from next door, I could see little craters starting to appear in the delicate white metal.

"Oh, Flan!" SBB wailed into the phone. "Now I'm having second thoughts, because if I live in the pod, the paparazzi will know exactly where to find me! Maybe if the pod were at the center of a maze . . ."

"Or you could live in your house," I suggested, trying not to roll my eyes. Being Sara-Beth's best friend required a lot of patience sometimes. "It's got plenty of places you can hide. Like the walk-in closets, and the guest room . . ."

"Hmm, that's a good point." The pod was bobbing in the air again, but Sara-Beth just waved it away.

"Flan, you're so good at pointing out angles no one's thought of. Have *you* ever considered interior design?"

"Umm . . ." I had enough problems without adding redecorating SBB's town house to the list. "Some things are better left to the professionals, I think."

"True, true." Sara-Beth ran to her roof's edge and yelled at the crane operator, "Take it back! I don't want it anymore!"

The pod sank back down to the street with a groan, and I could see the operator shouting angrily into his walkie-talkie. Oblivious to the chaos she'd caused, Sara-Beth sat down cross-legged on the roof in obvious relief.

"What a wonderful night for stargazing! I can see all three stars." She sighed dreamily. "So tell me what's been going on with you, sweetie?"

"Way too much." I looked at my jack-o'-lantern, with its crazy triangular eyes, and tucked my legs under me on the chair. Suddenly I felt totally exhausted. "I just wish things would go back to normal—or normal by Flood family standards, at least."

"Don't I know it. What I wouldn't give to live on a soundstage again!" SBB reached one arm upward, almost as though she were trying to pet one of the stars or maybe some imaginary sound boom.

I furrowed my brow. "But Sara-Beth, I thought you hated *Mike's Princesses*. You said it traumatized you for life."

"I wasn't talking about that. Anyway, tell me what's wrong, Flan. You know you can always rant to me."

I sighed. "Feb's just being really weird. She's trying to control everything I do!"

"Well, you know how I feel about those psychos in my family. Get a good lawyer as fast as you can!" Sara-Beth paused thoughtfully. "I know you can divorce your parents, but divorcing your sister might be a little trickier. Not impossible—but challenging."

"I don't want to divorce her. I just want her to be reasonable. I love her, but she's the flakiest person I know, and she's definitely in no position to give me advice." I leaned forward and rested my chin on my free palm. "I'm the one who goes to school every day, does my homework, and goes to bed before five A.M. It's so hypocritical. And even Patch is on the 'ground Flan' bandwagon now."

"Well . . ." Sara-Beth's voice took on the mysterious tone she always uses when quoting great philosophers or reading from the back of a Celestial Seasonings green tea box. "If there's one thing that awful Nada taught me, it's that there's a cosmic logic to the universe."

I watched the crane drive away, still holding the swinging bio-pod, and I couldn't help but wonder if the whole world was going crazy.

"Yeah, maybe."

"Like, you just saved me from living in a tiny pod!" Sara-Beth yelled, and then she started laughing, and I knew it was going to take forever to cool her down.

Chapter 13

JUST ANOTHER FABULOUS AFTERNOON WITH MY FABULOUS FRIENDS

There was no way I was going actually going to follow any of Feb's ridiculous rules, so after school on
Thursday, Meredith, Judith, and I took a cab to the
Meatpacking District to meet my other friends Liesel,
Philippa, and Sara-Beth Benny for tapas and drinks
at the Gansevoort Hotel. The hotel is one of the most
glamorous in New York. It's on this picturesque
cobblestone street and is fourteen stories tall. There
are windows everywhere, and it kind of looks like a
silver palace. Plus it has a rooftop deck and pool,
where you can look out over the entire city and see the
low buildings of the Village and Chelsea, the high-rises
of Midtown, and even the Empire State Building.

When we stepped into Ono, the Gansevoort's
Japanese restaurant, the other girls were already there,
sitting on a couple of minimalist gray silk couches in
a corner. The low table in front of them was covered

with little colorful plates and drinks the color of pink lip gloss.

"Flan!" Sara-Beth Benny leapt up. She was wearing a crocheted top with long fringe all over. She flung her arms around me, and a bunch of royal-purple strands hit me in the face. She usually wears a wig when she goes out, but apparently that afternoon at the Gansevoort, she felt comfortable enough to sit out in the open, more or less. Her hair was tied back in a purple scarf that matched her top, and her oversize Krizia sunglasses only covered half her face.

"I was so worried you wouldn't come!" she cried, finally letting go of me. I kissed Liesel and Philippa on both cheeks and took a seat next to SBB.

"Why wouldn't I?" I asked, setting down my Isabella Fiore schoolbag. "I just talked to you on the phone an hour ago."

"I know, but these last few days everyone's been letting me down! I just had to audition for a new TV pilot. Can you believe that? I've haven't had to audition for anything in *ages*! It was so awful. And I was just telling everybody about this nightmare I had about living in a pod—and you were in the dream, Flan!"

I kept quiet right then, rather than freak out SBB even more by telling her that her dream was real.

"Well, it sounds pretty exciting to me," Judith said as she and Meredith took a seat next to Liesel on a brown silk couch. "Definitely better than bio homework."

When I'd first met Judith and Meredith, they were obsessed with celeb gossip and tabloids, and I'd figured I needed to keep them separate from SBB, Philippa, and Liesel. Don't get me wrong: Meredith and Judith are both very cool, but when I first started at Stuy, they were a lot shyer, and I worried a lot they'd feel out of place with the Page Six crowd I'd grown up around. Now, though, they seemed perfectly at home at the Gansevoort on a Thursday afternoon. And I secretly hoped hanging out with non-Stuy people would create a sort of Adam-free zone.

"Excited about auditioning? At this point in my career? Ha!" A waitress appeared to take our orders. "I'll have another Death in the Afternoon." Sara-Beth sighed. Meredith, Judith, and I asked for virgin passion-fruit daiquiris.

"Don't sweat it, SBB. It's probably just a formality. You'll totally get the part." Philippa took a sip of her Bellini as Liesel nodded in agreement.

Liesel, Philippa, and SBB are all older than us—seniors in high school—and I met them through my brother, Patch. He and his friends (whom everybody calls the Insiders) know just about everybody who's anybody in Manhattan private schools, and Liesel and Philippa are two of the coolest girls in their clique. Liesel already works in PR, promoting trendy new bars and restaurants, which means she can always get us into the hottest clubs in town. She's a really cool person, and earlier in the semester she helped me plan a great party at my house, which I still owed her for big time. That night, her golden hair was poufed up at the forehead, and she was wearing a Nanette Lepore dress with a gold Chanel chain necklace and matching metallic handbag.

"What's been going on with you, Liesel? Any new parties coming up?" I asked.

"Nothing as exhausting as Sara-Beth's troubles, thank goodness." Liesel, who had been touching up her lipstick, snapped her MAC compact shut with a click and dropped it back into her bag. "But I'm so excited for Halloween. I'm organizing a benefit gala at MoMA, and it's going to be just sublime. Right now, we're still sorting out the entertainment. I wanted to hire Leland Brinker and his new band, but he refuses to play 'Monster Mash.' No matter what I say he just can't see the irony in it."

"That sucks." I used to have the biggest crush on

Leland, and he and Sara-Beth Benny had actually had some sort of romance, way back when he was still performing songs as Aladdin at Disneyland. I was kind of afraid that hearing his name might upset her, but she was too busy gulping down her cocktail to notice.

"MoMA's an amazing place for a party," Meredith said to Liesel. "I was there a few weeks ago with my art class, and an ambient improv group was playing in the big open area on the first floor. I practically started dancing around there myself."

"Well, I'm definitely ready for a good party," Philippa said as she adjusted her slouch cowboy boots. Philippa is just awesome—smart and laid-back, with a really great ironic sense of humor. She looks a little like Jennifer Connelly, only younger and taller, and that afternoon she was wearing Citizens jeans, a long black sweater, and four different necklaces. "I've been holed up in my room filling out college applications." She rolled her eyes. "I don't know how they expect us to have all these 'memorable experiences' if we're supposed to be stuck inside all day writing essays. Speaking of which, the three of us are going to a party for one of the Pussycat Dolls at Marquis later tonight. You guys want to come along?"

"Sorry." I pointed at my bulging schoolbag. "I

know it's almost the weekend, but I have way too much homework." I didn't bother to bring up my new "curfew."

"I hear ya. I'm really just procrastinating." Philippa tucked a strand of light brown hair behind her ear. The last time I'd seen her it had been dyed some weird burgundy color. I was glad she'd let it go natural again.

"How's Mickey?" I asked. Her boyfriend, Mickey Pardo, is one of my brother's best friends, but I hadn't seen him around for a while. In general, he's hard to miss, since he's always doing crazy stuff.

"Oh, he's all right," she said, sipping her Bellini. She speared a ginger shrimp with one of her chopsticks. "Relatively uninjured. Did you hear about his latest incident?"

I helped myself to a piece of sashimi. "No!"

She swallowed. I could tell she was trying not to smile. "He crashed his Vespa . . . into the back of an ice cream truck."

"No way!"

"Yeah, well, he wanted a Fudgesicle, and he saw the ice cream truck way up ahead, so he started speeding toward it. Then the truck hit a red light—and Mickey hit the truck." She shook her head. "Sometimes I just don't know what to do with the guy. Fortunately, he and the bike survived. With a few scratches. Enough about my love life." She turned to Judith. "How's yours? Meet anyone special lately?"

Judith blushed. "No, not really."

"Oh, c'mon. I bet you have."

Meredith looked over at her quickly, and then she started blushing too.

"There's a football game we're all not going to this weekend," Meredith said.

"Why?" Liesel asked. "The hottest guys are always on the football team. You should totally go!"

"I don't know . . ." I, Judith said. But she and Meredith were both staring at me like that decision was completely up to me.

Chapter 14

That Friday was so unseasonably warm and gorgeous that during our free period, Meredith, Judith, and I—along with practically everyone else at Stuyvesant—decided to go up on the roof to sit in the sun. I love the roof. With its wrought-iron chairs and matching glass-top tables, it's pretty much the perfect place to hang out with friends, eat hummus sandwiches, and, of course, people-watch. There's a nice tall ledge, so you never feel like you're going to fall off, and it's far enough away from the street that it's not too noisy. Plus, you can practically see all of Lower Manhattan from up there.

On the way up the stairs from the seventh floor, the three of us passed a crowd of cheerleaders coming down, all wearing red-and-blue uniforms and shrieking with laughter. Right behind them was a kid wearing a football jersey made out of red and blue duct tape. As soon as we stepped out onto the roof, I saw that a couple of guys had set up a card table. They had stethoscopes and lab notebooks, and they were poking and prodding at a football player sitting in a folding chair in front of them. Beside them on the table was a science fair backboard. DOES FOOTBALL INCREASE HEART RATE? it asked in giant letters.

"This is totally out of control," I said. "The whole school has football fever."

"Well, the first game *is* tomorrow," Judith pointed out. We walked over to an empty patch of roof, and she spread out the picnic blanket she'd brought up from her locker. "It's a pretty big deal."

"Maybe we should check it out. You know, just in the name of school spirit," Meredith said. "I mean, besides our old softball team, I've never really gone to any big games. I think it'd be fun."

"*I've* always liked football," said Judith. "If I don't get into Harvard, I'm definitely going to a Big Ten school."

"I'll go to the game with you guys," I told them. "But no more fighting over you-know-who."

Judith shook her head innocently. "You can barely even see the players way down on that field."

"Besides, they all look the same in their uniforms," Meredith agreed.

"Okay," I said. "I guess it'll be fun. But seriously, no more drama."

Meredith and Judith looked pleased—maybe a little too pleased—but they only exchanged one quick, suspicious glance before the three of us settled down to study a little bit for our classes later in the day. I decided that maybe this wouldn't be such a total disaster. After all, how were they supposed to get over Adam if they stayed cooped up dreaming about him all weekend? Getting out to the football game might even help. I was flipping through my biology textbook, looking at pictures of baby frogs and daydreaming about Bogie, when all of a sudden both my friends gasped.

"What?" I asked, startled. But it should have been obvious. The sun was in my eyes, but I could still see who they were staring at. Surprise, surprise, it was Adam—but even I'd never seen him looking quite like this. I guess he and a couple of his friends had just come from the pool down on the ground floor, because they were wearing swim trunks and flip-flops and sitting around on these big multicolored beach towels that looked like they belonged out on Coney Island or something. Adam was smiling and laughing, shaking water out of his curly hair. I'd never noticed before that he had a tan, but he did. He was practically golden.

For a second, I was just as speechless as they were. Then I rolled my eyes. I'd been giving this guy way too much credit. Who tans at school? And at the end of October, no less? An arrogant meathead, that's who. My friends were crazy to be pining over some jock who jumped at the chance to strip off his shirt—he had nice abs, sure, but that was no excuse for being vain.

"Oh my God," Judith breathed, clearly hypnotized by Adam's six-pack. She smiled sweetly and, leaning in front of Meredith, batted her eyes in his direction.

"Judith! Come on! *NAR!* You promised!" Meredith yanked Judith out of the way, then leaned forward herself, blocking her friend. She tossed her hair and cast Adam what she probably imagined was an impassioned, soulful gaze.

I waved my arms like I was stopping traffic. "Whoa, whoa, whoa. Come on. You're both way out of line. Forget about this guy already."

But the minute the words were out of my mouth, Adam looked over at us. His eyes skimmed over Meredith and Judith, then stopped at me. He smiled, and it was such a gentle, friendly smile that for a second I couldn't say anything. Then he hopped up and took two big strides and there he was, all of him, right in front of us.

"Hey, Flan," he said, towering over our blanket. His shadow fell over our books. "Hey, you guys."

"Hey," Meredith and Judith murmured in unison, their eyes wide.

I awkwardly stood up. "What's up?"

"I was just wondering—do we have to turn in any lab reports today for Bogie?" He smelled liked chlorine.

"No, I don't think so."

"Cool. Because I didn't get a chance to type up my log entries last night."

"No, don't worry about it." I raked my hand through my hair. Up close, Adam looked less like some lame lifeguard from a soap opera and more like some kind of mythological sun creature. When he smiled again, his teeth were blindingly white.

"Well, thanks," he said. He saluted Meredith and Judith. "Catch you guys later."

"Later," Meredith and Judith murmured in unison. As soon as he started walking back, they both stared at me, their mouths forming little *O*'s of surprise.

"What was *that* all about?" Judith asked.

I picked up my cell phone and pretended to inspect it. There was a text message from Bennett asking if Feb had been mad about last night. I closed it again. "What was what all about."

"He *smiled* at you," said Meredith. "Adam

McGregor smiled at you. And then he looked at you with his sensitive eyes like he knew your very soul."

"Oh, Meredith, he did not!" I reached up and touched my cheeks, which were kind of flushed.

"Well, he checked you out, that's for sure." Judith stared at me accusingly. "Why didn't you tell us you were friends?"

"He wasn't checking me out, Judith. And we're not friends. We're lab partners." I tapped my textbook like it was evidence for my case. "For biology."

"He's your lab partner?" they both squeaked in unison.

I slapped my forehead. "Look, I didn't want to tell you because I knew you guys would flip out. Now stop it, okay? You promised. And grilling me about this guy totally counts as breaking the No Adam Rule."

"Sure, and having joint custody of a tadpole doesn't?" Judith grumbled.

"Judith, we're sharing a microscope, not a martini at the Carlyle." I said with finality.

Meredith let out a little lovesick sigh, and they both went back to their homework. I set the biology text-book aside—I'd already spent way too much time thinking about Bogie the tadpole and, yes, Adam— and picked up my English book instead. I flipped to the assigned story, but before I even got through the first page, Meredith asked, a little too casually, "So, has Adam talked at all about what kind of books he likes to read? Just out of curiosity?"

"Meredith . . ." I warned her.

"I was just wondering, that's all," she said defensively. "I mean, for future reference, I want to know if I'm a good judge of what a guy is like. It seemed to me like he had the heart of a poet, so I was just wondering if I was right."

I rolled my eyes. Heart of a poet? She needed to stop renting all those costume dramas from the video store.

"Listen, it's not like he's poured his heart out to me. Mainly we just study this frog, okay? And he's not making up haikus on the spot about its webbed feet or the flakes of food we feed it."

Meredith looked back at her economics worksheet so sadly that I almost told her about how much Adam liked Hemingway and old movies. But it would've only encouraged her to obsess about him more.

"While we're on the subject of Adam—and for the record, I didn't bring it up," Judith added sharply to Meredith, who had just opened her mouth to protest, "I was just wondering if you two ever talked about me."

This time I refused to look up from my book. "No, Judith, we haven't."

"Now, come on. I'm not going to make a big deal about it. I just want to know what he said about me. For my own peace of mind." She tucked a pencil behind one ear. "I'd appreciate your honesty."

"Okay. Honestly, we've never talked about you. Not even once. If something's not green and slimy, you can pretty much bet we've never discussed it."

Judith looked crestfallen. "He never asked about me? Doesn't he know we're friends? Because when he talked to me about the weather that time, it seemed like he *really* wanted—"

I shook my head emphatically. It's always so weird talking to Meredith and Judith about guys. They always have these elaborate love affairs going on in their daydreams, and then they act all confused when, in real life, the guy in question has no clue what's going on. Not only had Adam never asked me about Judith, but I kind of doubted he even remembered their supposedly meaningful conversation. That seemed like a pretty harsh thing to point out, so I decided to change the subject instead. I stood up and looked down over the ledge of the roof, into the street below. A bunch of the shops and apartment buildings had haystacks and jack-o'-lanterns sitting on their stoops. One creative person had balanced a papier-mâché witch on a broomstick out on the rail of a fire escape.

"I can't believe it's almost Halloween already," I said. "Are you guys going to the Halloween parade?"

Fortunately for me, Meredith took the bait right away. "Oh, absolutely. My mom and grandma have been taking me every year since I was little. They get tons of ideas for designs from the costumes."

"We should all go to the parade together this year," I suggested. "Judith? You in?"

Judith set down her calculator. She still looked peeved, but she tried to match Meredith's enthusiasm. "Sure. It'll be . . . fun."

As the two of them started talking about what kind of costumes we should wear—fishnets and smoky eye makeup seemed to figure into every ensemble—I let myself sneak one last look at Adam. He was drinking neon green Gatorade from a bottle, and his hair had almost dried in the sunshine. I tried to tell myself that I was keeping Meredith and Judith away from him for their own good, but it was hard not feeling like a hypocrite. Who was I to enforce the No Adam Rule when I was developing a soft spot for the guy myself?

Chapter 15

*B*right and early Saturday morning I went off to go shopping with SBB. Since she moved in next door, it's kind of become a tradition of ours. At first, she needed things for the house—like towels and bath mats and sheets—because she considered everything from her old apartment to be contaminated with bad energy and allergens and other things that made her wake up screaming from nightmares. More recently, she's needed clothes for photo shoots, new sunglasses, and a pillbox to hold all her anti-anxiety drugs, which she stopped taking a week later because she said she "couldn't think." That morning, though, we were shopping for the most fun thing of all: Halloween costumes.

I figured we'd go to someplace like Halloween Adventure or Abracadabra Superstore, but Sara-Beth Benny had other plans.

117

"I'm sure those places are super, super cute, Flan, but they sell fake barf and whoopee cushions. And those little black-and-white saddle shoes like Gwen Stefani used to wear when she was still in No Doubt." SBB shivered at the memory.

"So where are we going?" I asked.

"Let's try Ina first—they have the best vintage clothing. Wouldn't it be wild if I were a zombie queen from the seventies?" Sara-Beth checked her BlackBerry. "Oh my God, this is horrible, horrible, horrible!" She frantically pushed little buttons as we walked along Perry Street.

"What is it?" I asked.

"It's just too terrible for words!" Somehow, this didn't stop Sara-Beth from rapidly typing on her tiny keypad. "My new decorator, Yvette St. Lucien, hasn't been able to find the watered silk curtains I wanted. She's been searching all over Paris!"

"Paris?" I asked as we turned onto Bleecker. I peered into the Marc Jacobs accessory store—there was a cute elephant key chain in the window—and at the line of people waiting outside Magnolia for cupcakes.

"Of course. You know, I didn't realize this until a couple of days ago, but did you know that if you want really high-quality materials, you have to go over to

Europe and get them yourself? Yvette explained the whole thing to me, so of course I put her on the next plane. But now it looks like it's all been a big waste of time!" Sara-Beth scrutinized her little screen. "Oh, wait, she just texted me. Wait . . . wait . . . she found them after all!" She shut off her BlackBerry and held one hand to her forehead, like she was about to swoon. "This is such a relief. I really didn't want to wait another week while she tromped all around Venice."

"Why do you want these curtains so much?" We passed a leafless tree that had cute mini pumpkins with painted smiley faces dangling from the branches.

"Well, I haven't seen them myself, because they only have them in certain very exclusive boutiques overseas, but Yvette tells me they're the very best— the same kind that were hanging in Versailles when Sofia Coppola shot her Marie Antoinette movie. And you have to trust a Frenchwoman in matters of taste— I mean, it's absolutely in their blood."

"Yvette is French?"

"I think so. Or French Canadian." She waved the question away with her birdlike hands. Then she grabbed my arm and pulled me along behind her as she made a beeline for Cynthia Rowley.

"What about Ina?" I gasped, trying to keep up. But

Sara-Beth just rushed over to a high-necked red silk dress that was hanging on the back wall.

"Isn't this hideous?" she shrieked. "Imagine it with stilettos. It's totally, totally something from the depths of hell."

"Can I help you?" a saleslady asked, stepping briskly from behind the counter. Her hair was swirled up into this kind of tornado of hairspray, and she had on such dark eye shadow that, even if she hadn't been glaring at us, she would've looked a little bit like an evil arch-villain from one of Bennett's favorite super-hero comics. After one look at her, I was ready to get out of there. But Sara-Beth had already veered over to another clothing rack.

"Thanks, we're just browsing," I said sheepishly, and slunk over to where Sara-Beth stood, pawing at a black-and-white patterned tube dress with multicol-ored ruffles around the middle.

"This is like something from my pod nightmare." She picked the hanger up and held the dress to herself for size. "It's absolutely schizophrenic! A psychotic clown suit."

"It seems like you ladies are looking for something in particular," said the salesgirl, following us across the room. Her arms were crossed, and I noticed that the top she had on was made from same fabric of the dress that had now reduced Sara-Beth to tears of laughter.

"We're just shopping for Halloween costumes," Sara-Beth exclaimed. "And it looks like you've got a whole store full of them. Ooh!" She seized a white pleated skirt from a nearby clothing rack and swung it around, making ghost noises.

"I'm afraid we don't carry anything like that," the salesgirl said, touching the oversize beads of her chunky rainbow-colored necklace.

"You must be joking! This place is insane!" Sara-Beth spotted something else she wanted to look at—probably a metallic silver minidress that looked a little like a skimpy spacesuit—but the saleslady stepped in her way before she could dart over to grab it.

"You might want to try another establishment." The girl smiled, fake-nice and condescending. "There's a Duane Reade down the street. If you hurry, they might have some Dora the Explorer outfits left."

"Excuse me? Do you even know who I am?" For someone who's always hiding from the paparazzi, Sara-Beth asks that question a lot. She straightened up, draping the little white skirt over her arm. But either the saleslady didn't know or didn't care. She gave Sara-Beth a once-over.

"Actually," she said, "I take that back. You don't need a costume at all. You can just wear light brown and go as a toothpick."

Sara-Beth burst into tears. "You horrible, horrible woman! How dare you make fun of my metabolism! Come on, Flan, let's get out of here!"

The saleslady smirked. I shot her a nasty look as I followed Sara-Beth out of the store.

"How could she speak to me like that?" she demanded, storming down the street. Trying to keep up with her, I almost tripped over someone's little dachshund. "It's not my fault I have small bones!"

"She was pretty awful," I agreed. Sara-Beth had been loud and kind of rude, but the toothpick remark was still totally uncalled-for.

"I eat! I eat all the time!" Sara-Beth looked at me angrily, as if daring me to contradict her. "Come on, Flan, let's get a cupcake right now!"

So the two of us walked down the street to Magnolia Bakery. I could already smell the sugar from half a block away. Magnolia Bakery is a really cute bakery, and they're open pretty late—more than once I'd been there at eleven-fifteen, waiting in line with February for an icebox cake and two coffees. Of course, that was before she became a total psycho dictator over my personal life. Anyway, Magnolia Bakery is famous for its cupcakes, which are sweet and fluffy and just about everything you can hope for. They're so popular there's actually a limit of one dozen per person. We grabbed two pale pink–frosted ones from the counter and paid.

As we turned the corner onto West Eleventh Street, Sara-Beth still seemed upset about the toothpick remark, so I started talking about whatever I could think of to take her mind off it. I started describing Bogie, the tadpole, and how cute he was with his bugged-out eyes and weird little tail, how he bumped his nose up against the side of the jar when he wanted to say hello, and how I thought he'd already started to recognize Adam and me. Which got me talking about Adam and how good he was with animals, and how now even Bennett thought he was a great guy—which was great, sort of, but kind of weird too. Before I knew it, I was complaining about how Meredith and Judith were so obsessed with him that it was practically destroying their friendship.

"I mean, they keep acting all competitive with each other—they were even jealous of me, just because Adam and I were saying hi to each other up on the roof. It's totally out of control. Really, no guy is worth throwing away your friendship over. Even if he is handsome . . . and friendly . . . and athletic . . . and, okay, funny and generous and good with animals—there's still no way *I'd* ever go after someone like him if it meant ditching Meredith and Judith. Even if he does like to read and watch old movies . . ."

I trailed off, because Sara-Beth Benny had stopped in her tracks. For a second, I thought she'd spotted a paparazzo and we were going to have to run and hide behind a parked car or something. But instead she just stared at me. She'd taken one bite of her cupcake, but now she let the rest of it fall dramatically into the street.

"Oh. My. God," she said.

"What?" I finished my cupcake and wiped icing from my lips.

"Flan, why didn't you tell me?" Sara-Beth seized my arm. Her fingers dug into my skin.

"Why didn't I tell you what?"

"*You're* in love with Adam!"

"What? No way!" I protested.

"It's so obvious, I can't believe I didn't see it before." Sara-Beth threw her arms around me exuberantly. "I'm so sorry! I'm the first to admit that I can be a tiny bit self-involved. I've been so wrapped up in this decorating business. . . ."

I shook my head and tried to laugh it off. My heart was racing so fast I felt like it might explode. "Listen, Sara-Beth, I'm not in love with Adam. It just doesn't make any sense. I have a great boyfriend, remember? And Meredith and Judith—"

"Flan, you're so silly." Sara-Beth grabbed my hands. "Love is absolutely not supposed to make sense! It's crazy, crazy, crazy. That's why they call it love." She linked her arm through mine and began tugging me down the street. "Now I see we'll have to go a whole other direction with your costume—historical. You could be . . . oh, what's-her-name, King Arthur's wife."

"Guinevere," I said. I couldn't help smiling, imagining what kind of bizarre getup SBB would have me wear.

"Yes, that's her!" She smiled dreamily. "And Adam can be your knight in shining armor. Or you could be that other one, that poor Russian lady who threw herself on the train tracks for love. I know a wonderful, wonderful makeup artist who can make it look exactly like your head was severed and reattached. It's mostly a question of fake blood and glue and railroad spikes . . . unless you'd rather be that pilgrim lady from *The Scarlet Letter*!"

I laughed. "I'm not sure I want to wear buckles on my shoes all night."

"Ooh, and they had those ugly bonnets, too. Good thinking, Flan—we need to make you look cute. But, anyway, this will be so much fun."

As Sara-Beth kept chattering, I bit my lip and stared into the windows of the stores we were passing. Even an eyeglass outlet had a Halloween-themed display. I was glad SBB was wrong about Adam and me, because if I did have a crush on him, the holiday would be a total disaster. So would the rest of the school year, most likely.

Sara-Beth and I wandered all over the place looking for dresses. After about four hours of searching, she finally found a crazy black, Renaissance-fair-looking gown at this awesome punk place, Trash and Vaudeville, in the East Village. And even though they were covered with safety pins and tattoos, the salespeople there were a million times friendlier than the lady in Cynthia Rowley. They suggested a good alterations place where we could go to get Sara-Beth's dress made small enough, and they even took her picture to hang on the wall before we left the shop.

Sara-Beth was meeting Philippa and Liesel at the Rose Bar up by Gramercy Park for drinks, and I had to get home to get ready for the football game, so we split up around six o'clock. But as I climbed the steps to my town house, I was still thinking about our conversation. I'd tried to laugh it off, but it was really starting to bother me. Did I like Adam?

As a friend, of course. Yes, he was charming and

definitely cute, but it was Bennett, with his great sense of humor and his hipster tastes, who was perfect for me. Sure I was curious about what costume Adam would choose for Halloween, but it was Bennett who I actually wanted to hang out with on Halloween . . . right?

Chapter 16

*M*eredith, Judith, and I were meeting that night at the stadium. I'd e-mailed Bennett about the plan and he'd written back that he'd come by around seven to pick me up. When I came to the door, he was wearing a leprechaun T-shirt that said KISS ME, I'M IRISH.

"Hey, Bennett," I said, grabbing Noodles before he careened out of the house. "You want to come in for a second?"

"No, we better get going. You have everything?"

"Sure." I glanced into the hallway mirror and gave myself a quick once-over. I hadn't gotten a Halloween costume yet, but I had bought some new clothes. When we were wandering around SoHo, Sara-Beth had insisted we go into Betsey Johnson, and I'd bought a cute new dress, which was teal with little yellow roses all over it. I'd also gotten this fuzzy yellow sweater from an awesome little vintage shop just a few blocks away from my house. At first, I figured my new outfit wouldn't look too dressy for a football game if I wore sneakers, but then I decided I might as well wear my heels too. I'd gotten all dressed up, but then, fortunately, sanity had reclaimed me at the last minute, and I'd changed into jeans and a Stuy tank top, but I decided to keep on my strappy sandals . . . just in case. I shrugged on a blue cardigan and grabbed my purse. "What's up?"

"Not too much." He noticed my tank top. "Hey, that's awesome. School spirit."

"Yeah, totally." I rolled my eyes. Judging from the way he'd reacted to the pep rally, I figured he was being sarcastic. "I hope you don't mind me dragging you to this game. I know sports aren't really your thing."

"You're not dragging me. Actually, after talking to Adam the other day, I switched my assignment at the paper to the sports column for this week. My first article will be about tonight's game."

"Wow." I looked over at him in surprise, but he was dead serious. We reached the Fourteenth Street subway station and made our way down the puddly concrete steps—somehow subway stops are always drippy and wet even when it's not raining. Bennett swiped me through the metal turnstile with his MetroCard, and we walked along the platform, waiting for the next 1 train to come.

"Yeah. You know, Adam's pretty cool. We've e-mailed back and forth a couple of times, and I might be going over to his apartment later this week to hang out with him and his brother. They have a Wii." We stopped walking and Bennett leaned against a steel girder with peeling yellow paint. He looked thoughtful. "I guess he just seems a lot smarter than I expected a football player to be. Nicer, too." The train rumbled into the station, and Bennett raised his voice over the noise. "I've been doing some research for my article, and the amount of strategy involved is really kind of fascinating."

When we arrived at the stadium, it was like the pep rally times a thousand. The place was teeming with people, and concession stands selling hot dogs, nachos, and soda were overwhelmed with long lines of teenagers. The walls and floors were concrete, and hand-painted posters were taped up everywhere. A GO PEGLEGS! sign was hanging from a kiosk some enterprising Stuy students had set up to sell eye-patches, armbands, and knit hats with pictures of Pegleg Pete embroidered on them. When it was our turn in line, Bennett bought an armband for me.

"You're so sweet, Bennett. You didn't have to do

that," I said, sliding it up on my arm. He kissed the top of my head.

"It looks cute on you."

We let the crowd pull us along into the stadium. I squinted, glancing around for Meredith and Judith, then looked down at the football field. The cheerleaders were turning cartwheels and forming pyramids and spelling out VICTORY, and behind them some guy in a gigantic foam pirate head was dancing around. The band had set up down on the field, and they were playing "Louie Louie" at top volume. The musicians were so into it that some of them were swinging their tubas and saxophones in time to the music. Already, the crowd was getting riled up, and even though I'm really more used to ballet and Broadway musicals than I am to sports games, it wasn't hard to get in the spirit. People were doing the wave, and we got up and sat down twice before we even had a chance to make sure we were in the right seats. We were sitting fairly close, but the football field was farther away than I'd imagined, and I started to wonder if Adam would even be able to see us from so far away before I checked myself and put the thought out of my mind.

"There they are," said Bennett, pointing down at the crowd filing into the stadium. I almost started laughing; the way they were dressed definitely made me glad I'd changed clothes. Meredith had on a halter-neck dress with little flowers patterned all over it, with white patent leather heels and pink fabric roses in her hair. Judith was wearing a striped bubble skirt and a tight, low-cut black sweater she'd bought the other day at Bebe. Halos of black eyeliner framed her chocolate brown eyes. The two of them spotted us and hurried up the bleachers, elbowing each other to get there first.

"Hey, great seats," said Judith, stretching her legs out onto the bleachers in front of her so no one could block her view of the star QB. She smoothed her hair, inspected the field, then quickly took her compact out of her purse to check her makeup.

"How're you two doing?" Meredith asked, leaning in front of Judith to see us. Judith pushed her away.

"You guys look fancy," I said. "What's the occasion?"

"Didn't you hear about the after-party?" Judith swiped on some lipstick and shut her mirror. "Everyone's going to be there." She stared into my eyes significantly. "Everyone."

"Not me," said Bennett.

"Oh no, really?" I asked.

"Yeah, unfortunately Mr. Neil, our teacher advisor, wants to look over all our articles before they go to press on Sunday. So I've got to e-mail it to him tonight." Bennett noticed my disappointed expression. "Hey, don't worry. You guys'll have fun without me. There'll be lots of cool people there. You know, like Adam."

Meredith, Judith, and I all fell into a deep, awkward silence.

"Hey, look. Eric and Jules." Bennett stood up and waved to his friends. They scaled the stairs and came over to us. Jules was holding a tray of nachos; Eric looked perfectly manicured in a brown turtleneck sweater and a pair of tan slacks. When we'd first met them, Judith had considered Eric the cutest guy in tenth grade, but now she hardly batted an eye in his direction. It made me kind of sad; why were Meredith and Judith both fixating on Adam where there were perfectly nice guys right here in front of them?

"Hey, what's up?" Bennett asked his friends. "I didn't know you guys were coming."

"I don't think we'll stay," Jules explained. "I got press passes to take pictures for the school paper, but when I got here they told me they already have a team of professionals working on it. Which is really just as well—I don't particularly want to be down there on the field without a helmet. Hey, Meredith."

"Oh. Hi, Jules." Meredith broke her concentration

on the football field for a second to give him a quick smile. His eyes lingered on her, and after a second he cleared his throat to speak again.

"I've been wanting to tell you, I read that book of Beat poetry you recommended. It was really something."

"Really?" She turned her head to one side, surprised, and for a second I swore she was crushing on him again. But then it was gone, and her eyes drifted back toward the football field, where the cheerleaders were throwing each other into the air. "I'm thinking of writing some poetry myself," she added absently. I had a sneaking suspicion that I knew who the inspiration might be.

Eric looked bored and slightly annoyed that Judith was ignoring him, too. "You know what? Let's get out of here," he said to Jules. To the rest of us, he announced. "Football's overrated."

The two of them pushed back down the big concrete steps, past the hordes of people still flooding into the stadium. Jules stopped once to look back at Meredith, but she was too busy watching Adam to notice.

Out of the four of us, Judith was the only one who'd watched a whole football game before, so she had to explain the game, play by play, for about the first twenty minutes. I'm not sure how much it helped, though, because about half of her sentences trailed off when she caught a glimpse of Adam down on the field, doing something athletic and heroic looking. As quarterback, he was at the center of the offensive action: throwing passes, running at top speed, even getting tackled, which made all three of us gasp and leap to our feet.

"You guys are really getting into this," observed Bennett, jotting down some notes in his Captain America notebook. "Maybe we'll all be sports fans by the end of the season."

Bennett was right: I hadn't been expecting to care about it nearly so much, but practically the whole time, I was on the edge of my seat. During halftime, I realized that my throat was sore from all the cheering, so when Meredith went to the concession stand, I gave her money to buy me a Coke. The minute she left her seat, though, a guy in a Space Camp T-shirt and wraparound sunglasses came over and stood awkwardly in the aisle, staring at us.

"Hey there, Judy," he called in a strange, nasally voice.

Judith looked at me with an "oh my God" expression, but I just shrugged. I had no idea who he was. She turned back toward him with a forced-looking smile.

"Hi, Kelvin," she called back.

"Mind if I sit here till your friend gets back?" He picked his way between the seats and plunked down next to her, then waved over at us. "Heyyy." When he smiled, I could see he had glow-in-the-dark green rubber bands on his braces.

"Hey," I said.

"Flan, this is Kelvin, my lab partner from bio," Judith said with a desperate, "get this guy away from me" gleam in her eyes.

"Have you guys been doing that amphibian life unit?" I asked politely.

"Yeah. Yeah, we sure have." Kelvin rubbed his hands together. "I can't wait till we do the dissection."

"The dissection? What?" I glanced over at Bennett anxiously. He shrugged.

"Yeah, the dissection. When you get to slice the frog's skin off and label all its nerve fibers with push-pins. Heh heh." He wheezed and wiggled his fingers in delight. "I've been practicing with a digital imaging program on my computer, and some of the models I've made are pretty badass. Did you know some toads have jewels in their backs?"

"I'm not going to dissect my tadpole!" I thought of my little Bogie, swimming around in his jar so trustingly. Maybe I was crazy, but I could have sworn that Bogie was really starting to love and depend on me. His little frog lips always seemed to curve in an adoring amphibian smile when I took him off the shelf in bio. Then at the end of class, when I had to put him back, he seemed to look longingly at me, as though he wanted me to take him home. How could they expect me to treat him like an alien autopsy? "Bennett, when you took bio, did they make you do this?"

"I don't know. I took botany instead. Cutting up rose stems wasn't nearly so gruesome." Then he looked up from his notebook and saw that I was really upset. "Flan, I bet you can talk to the teacher about it. If you're really uncomfortable about it, maybe somebody else could do the incisions. Like Adam—he's your lab partner, so . . ."

"I don't want either of us to kill the frog! Why can't the poor thing just live a full life?" I felt almost ready to cry. "I won't do it! I can't!"

"I think we have to, Flan," said Judith. "It's part of the final."

Bennett threw his arm around me. "Don't worry, Flan," he murmured, stroking my back. "I'm sure we can figure something out."

I wanted to believe him, but all I could think about was how when I opened the jar to feed Bogie on

Friday, he had reached out with his little budding webbed hands and touched my finger.

When Meredith came back, creepy Kelvin finally had to leave her seat, and before too long, the game started again. It was a close one. By the final quarter, our team was down 13 to 17. It really looked like we were going to lose. I've always thought it was funny when Patch's friends yell at the TV during football games, but for the first time that evening, I really understood. Along with the rest of the stadium, Meredith, Judith, and I were on our feet, screaming at the top of our lungs, and I could feel my heart pounding, as if I was the one running back and forth across the Astroturf field. For a minute, the outcome of the game seemed like the most important thing in the world. But then something funny happened. Our coach called a time-out, and, as the players were jogging to the side of the field to have a huddle, Adam stopped for a minute to pull off his helmet. When he looked up again, it was straight at me. And even though he was way down there on the field, I swear our eyes met.

At the beginning of the next play, Adam had the ball in hand on the forty-yard line, with only twelve seconds left on the clock and the other team's whole defensive line right in front of him. He looked left, then right, and I thought he'd get tackled for sure. But just as a hulking linebacker barreled straight toward him, Adam gracefully leapt to the side. At the exact same moment, he threw the ball. The pass arced down the field like a giant rainbow and the whole stadium went silent. We were all transfixed by the ball. I looked at Adam and I could swear he was smiling as he watched his pass. Down in the end zone a receiver looked almost surprised as he jumped up, grabbed the ball to his chest, and fell to the ground.

Out in the stands, everyone went insane. "TOUCH-DOWN!" Meredith, Judith, and I screamed, giving each other high fives. Then we looked down at the field. Adam was holding his helmet in one hand, pointing it at us. Meredith and Judith practically swooned. I felt my face turning bright red. And it only got redder when I looked over and saw the confused expression on Bennett's face.

Chapter 17

I better get going," said Bennett, packing up his stuff. "This article's due in an hour and a half. Say congratulations to Adam for me, okay?"

"You're sure you don't want to split a cab with us?"

"Nah, I'll just take the subway." Bennett kissed me on the cheek. "Have a good time at the party. I'll call you tomorrow."

I gave him a big hug. "Happy writing."

Meredith, Judith, and I squeezed our way through the crowd of celebrating students and hailed a cab to Crockett's, the club where they were throwing the after party. Crockett's is this really cool underground lounge on the Upper West Side that's owned by a Stuy alum. It kind of reminds me of one of those speakeasies from the '20s: it's in a basement room with antique couches and tasseled lamps, and on some nights a jazz band comes in and plays on a little stage in the back.

Tonight, though, there was no live music, and even if there had been, we wouldn't have been able to hear it over the noise of the crowd. Practically everyone from school was there: at one point, I even thought I glimpsed one of the math teaching assistants drinking a pomegranate martini. The football players arrived a little less than an hour after we did—I guess they had to shower and change clothes—and when they walked through the door, I had to cover my ears, because the whole crowd cheered liked we were back in the stadium again.

At the front of the pack of players, Adam flashed a humble smile, and I thought Meredith and Judith were going to hyperventilate. He did look pretty cute—he'd put on a clean white shirt and a pair of khakis, and except for a little white bandage on one elbow, you'd never have known that he'd just spent the last few hours getting body-slammed by three-hundred-pound defensive ends. A week ago I would've scoffed at how everyone was congratulating him like he'd just been crowned king or something, but now I was cheering wildly along with everyone.

At first, everything was great. Loud hip-hop music blared from the speakers, and some people had started dancing up by the bar. I recognized a lot of faces and said hi to kids from my classes, which really made me feel like I was a part of the whole Stuy community. But things started to go downhill when we decided to order drinks—a Red Bull for me and Cokes for Meredith and Judith—and sat down at a free table by one of the windows.

"The game was so much fun! I'm glad we decided to go!" Meredith exclaimed, crunching on an ice cube.

Judith flipped her hair back. "Well, you're lucky I was there, because I was the only one who actually understood what was going on."

Meredith narrowed her eyes, "I really enjoyed connecting with the *poetry* of the game, which is way more important than the stupid rules."

"Right." Judith laughed condescendingly, pointing her red drink straw at Meredith for emphasis. "Because if you understand the *poetry* of a triangle, you'll pass a geometry test."

"You're just jealous because I felt the game on a different level from you." Meredith put her hand over her heart. "I had more of a *visceral* reaction to it all."

Judith snorted. "No offense, but I think you're being kind of pretentious. I mean, football's not about poetry or watercolors. It's about who wins and who loses."

"I don't care who wins or loses." Meredith

rummaged through her purse and pulled out her watermelon-flavored ChapStick. "I'm interested in who has the most passion."

I finished off my Red Bull with a gulp and said loudly, "You know, I think I'm ready to leave! Want to head out?"

Meredith and Judith agreed right away. I think the escalating tension was starting to freak them both out, too. But in a way, it was really weird: for all their obsessing over Adam, neither of them seemed too sad that they were leaving without talking to him. It was almost like he was a cute actor in a movie we'd just seen. It didn't really occur to them to go and try to hang out with him like he was a regular person.

I was so anxious to get them out of the club that I didn't realize I'd left my purse at the table until we were outside.

"You guys go on without me," I said. Meredith and Judith only lived a couple blocks away, so it wasn't like we were all going to split a cab anyway. "I'll see you in school on Monday."

"You sure, Flan?" Judith asked. "We could help you look for it."

"No, it's fine—it must be right under our table or somewhere nearby." I waved good-bye and headed back to the club.

Inside Crockett's, I picked my way through the crowd, sidestepping swaying classmates who'd clearly ordered drinks a teensy bit stronger than my Red Bull. In the few minutes I'd been gone, my table had been taken over by a bunch of empty shot glasses, salt-shakers, and chunks of half-eaten lime slices, but I didn't see my purse anywhere. Trying not to panic, I dropped down to my knees and peered under the table.

"Anything good down there?" a voice asked from above me.

Startled, I twisted around.

Adam. I quickly stood up and brushed off my jeans.

"I've been looking for you. Are you leaving already?" he said, leaning against the wall and grinning at me somewhat flirtatiously.

"Trying to." I tried to sound as unflirtatious as possible. "But I can't seem to find my purse."

"There's an easier way to look, you know." Adam brushed past me and effortlessly lifted the table off the floor, careful to keep the shot glasses balanced on top. Sure enough, I saw my purse immediately—it had been jammed between a chair leg and the wall—and reached down to pick it up.

"Thanks!" I checked to make sure nothing had fallen out of the bag.

"Happy to help." Adam set the table back down as

two giggling girls rushed past us and ducked into a bathroom. "So, did you enjoy the game?"

"Totally. The team did a great job. Especially you." It wasn't flirting if it was the truth, right? Just for good measure, I added, "Bennett told me to congratulate you, too. He was really sorry to miss this party."

"Well, at least you guys made it to the game. I knew you'd like football!"

"Yeah . . ." I bit my lip, suddenly feeling self-conscious because a couple of juniors had started to make out two feet away from us. Plus, Meredith and Judith would freak out if they knew I was talking to Adam after I suggested we all leave. "Well, I should probably head home. My sister's been on this psycho power trip recently, and I'm not exactly in the mood to get grounded."

Adam nodded. "I'll walk you out."

I started to protest, but he grabbed my hand and led me through the crowd to the door. Even though our conversation had been completely harmless, I felt shy and a little bit guilty, sure that the entire club was pointing and whispering about how the blond girl holding Adam's hand was a bad friend and girlfriend. But when I braved a glance around, I realized everyone was too wrapped up in dancing and celebrating even to notice us.

I dropped Adam's hand the second we stepped outside and crossed my arms in front of my chest. Adam followed me to the corner of Eighty-third and Amsterdam, and then nudged my foot with his. "Impressive you made it through the whole game in those. Aren't your feet cold?"

I looked down at my strappy sandals, and then made a face at him. "Hey, I wasn't the one hanging out in my swimsuit on the roof in October." Although I had to admit that Chloé heels *were* a little dressy for a high school football game.

Adam held his hands up in surrender. "Point taken. But don't blame me if you can't feel your toes on Monday in bio."

"My toes feel just fine, thank you." I wriggled my toes (which I had painted metallic red for the occasion) and hit him lightly on the arm. Okay, so maybe *harmless* wasn't the right word to describe our conversation—after all, why would any two people talk about toes in the middle of the street at night if there wasn't something else going on? If I were being honest with myself, I'd say we were flirting and just, well, accept it. But I shook off that reality and decided to strengthen my resolve and list all the reasons for the No Adam Rule.

I'd only gotten to reason number one (Bennett)

when Adam took a step toward me. He was so close I could smell his minty aftershave and see a tiny snag near the collar of his button-down shirt. And that was *it*. All thoughts of Bennett, Meredith, and Judith flew out of my mind, and I shut my eyes to kiss him. But as I heard a car brake behind me, I realized with searing embarrassment that Adam had stepped toward me—toward the curb—not to kiss me, but to flag down a passing cab.

"Um, thanks," I mumbled, praying he hadn't noticed me assume a pre-kiss pose.

My heart beating violently, I clumsily climbed in the back of the car and rested my head against the cracked leather of the seat. With one hand on the open cab door, Adam leaned across me so he could tell the cabdriver I was headed downtown. Before he stood up, his sea-green eyes found mine. In one quick motion, he brushed his lips against mine and whispered, "I'm really glad you came," before slamming the door shut.

As the cab rolled away to join the sea of red taillights driving along the avenue, I was left with only one thought: Whoa. *I am in trou-ble.*

"Where you headed exactly?" the cabdriver asked.

"Give me a moment," I said. "I'm not exactly sure."

Chapter 18

After what happened, I could barely think straight, so when the cab reached Perry Street, I did the only thing that made sense: I raced to Sara-Beth Benny's house and rang her bell. I heard the first few notes of "Frère Jacques" chime inside the house before she opened the door.

"Oh my God, Flan, I'm so glad to see you!" she exclaimed, yanking me inside by the arm. "Quick! The paparazzi have eyes on this place at all hours!"

I blinked, looking around. Once again, her apartment was unrecognizable. All traces of the opium den disaster had disappeared. Instead, I felt as though I had accidentally walked into one of those sections at the Metropolitan Museum that displays how Europeans decorated their houses in the 1700s, only without those velvet cords that prevent museumgoers from touching anything. Flowery pastel paper lined the walls, and delicate side chairs that looked like they'd come straight from Versailles itself stood in the corners of the room. On an antique end table sat a bunch of little painted ceramic figurines: a waltzing couple, a woman selling flowers, a little mime in whiteface holding a mandolin. An ornate, gilded mirror hung on one wall, and a large Impressionist-style painting of Sara-Beth Benny hung between two windows on another. In it, she wore a white powdered wig and smiled coyly behind an elaborately painted fan.

The real-life Sara-Beth, though, was skipping around all the antiques in her new living room, looking like she'd just escaped from the modern-art wing. She was wearing pajamas with silk-screened Andy Warhol Marilyn Monroes patterned all over them in crazy Day-Glo colors, and she had streaks of bright blue moisturizer under her eyes.

"What do you think?" she asked, flopping down on a pale pink satin settee positioned below a window. It looked pretty uncomfortable—overstuffed, with buttons pushing up through the upholstery. "Isn't it just so . . . rococo?"

"Rococo?" I repeated, sitting down on a weird little ottoman with claw-footed legs. "Yeah, I guess so."

"I think it's divine," said Sara-Beth, idly plucking at

the watered silk drapes hanging from the window behind her. They were a pretty powder blue color, but I wasn't sure they'd been worth a trip to Europe. "Yvette is absolutely inspired. Yesterday she found me a genuine cherrywood mantelpiece from an estate in the north of Spain!"

"But you don't have a fireplace," I pointed out. Looking around the cluttered room, I wondered where she could even put a mantel.

"Well, not yet. Oh, I haven't told you the big news!" Sara-Beth straightened up, clapping her hands together. "Do you remember that sublime director, Ric Roderickson? Well, he's thinking of filming an adaptation of some book called *Justine* in the south of France—a period piece, you know, an art movie—and there might be a part in it for me! Several parts, actually! Of course, if I were going to Europe, I'd have to send trunks and trunks on ahead, and of course you'd help me pack, wouldn't you? In fact, you could come along with me and we could go antiquing and find all kinds of amazing trinkets to put on my cherrywood mantel!" SBB stopped short and trained her electric-blue-ringed eyes on me. "Flanny, what's going on? You look . . . well, not very Flan-like!"

At that point, I burst into tears, and the whole story came pouring out—how Judith and Meredith were still fighting, how Feb and Patch were driving me nuts, how I cared about Bennett but couldn't stop thinking about Adam, who'd just kissed me.

"And the thing is," I concluded, still sniffling, "I just don't know what to do. I know people are going to get hurt no matter what I do, and I don't want to be the kind of person who hurts her friends. . . ." I trailed off, hugging a somewhat hard satin pillow to my chest.

"Oh, Flanny," SBB finally said. "Let me make you some tea."

She disappeared into the kitchen, and after about ten minutes of crashing around, she came back out with a slightly tarnished antique silver tea set on a platter. In place of cookies, she had a package of these weird wasabi rice crisps she's always eating.

"Now, drink this. You'll feel better," she said, pouring me a cup. I gratefully took it from her. Little men and women in shepherd costumes frolicked on the outside of my engraved silver cup.

"But what do you think I should do?" The tea was raspberry-lemon flavored, my favorite.

"I guess it all depends on who you like better," said Sara-Beth, putting a needlepoint throw pillow behind her head.

"But I don't know. I mean, Bennett's great. He's

cute, he's funny, he's really, really nice. He's totally the kind of boyfriend I always thought I'd have. I have way more in common with him than I do with . . . just about any other guy. Well, minus his comic book obsession."

"But . . . ?"

"But . . . I don't know. I'm like Meredith and Judith, I guess. I just have a stupid crush on Adam." I stared down at the rug. Sarah-Beth's decorator must have gotten it from some old royal family or something, because it was woven with gold threads and patterned all over with a coat of arms. "I really should just forget tonight ever happened."

Sara-Beth pursed her lips. "Really? Because honestly, Flan, when you got here tonight, you were glowing."

"I was?"

"Now, don't let me tell you what to do. But my personal philosophy is, if you see something you want, take it!" She gestured wildly with her cup, sloshing black raspberry tea onto the carpet.

"But what about the thing you said before? About how, if two friends want the same thing—like a guy or a part in a movie—they should agree not to go after it?"

Sara-Beth waved her hand dismissively. "Oh, Flan, that never works. It's absolutely impossible."

"Wait a minute. Didn't you and Ashleigh-Ann Martin keep the promise you made to stop auditioning for the same things? I thought you said that saved your friendship."

Sara-Beth laughed uproariously. "Saved our friendship?"

"Sure."

"Flanny, Flanny, Flanny—I haven't spoken to that Las Vegas trash in years!"

"What? But I thought—"

She tossed the needlepoint pillow on the floor and hugged herself, rocking back and forth with giggles. "Oh, sometimes you really are too cute!" She caught her breath and looked me square in the eye. "Flan, the reason that I'm a success and Ashleigh-Ann Martin is doing knife commercials at two in the morning is— well, there are a lot of reasons, actually, and let's just say that Tan in a Can isn't a good look for anyone. But *another* reason is that I knew what I wanted and I wasn't going to let someone else stand in the way of me getting it. And because my agent forced me—I mean, *forced* me, though of course I run my own life, you know that—to audition for *Paris in the Springtime* even though there was a teensy little possibility that Ashleigh-Ann might possibly think that meant I was breaking my promise."

"Well, I guess I'm going to have to think about this," I said, getting up. "Thanks, SBB. I'll call you tomorrow."

"Au revoir!" Sara-Beth called after me as I let myself out.

I took my keys out as I walked next door to my house, still thinking about everything that had gone wrong. Talking to Sara-Beth helped—she always knew how to cheer me up—but I still felt sick about what had happened. What kind of a friend was I? I didn't even trust myself, or my own feelings, anymore.

It was almost one in the morning, but I figured if I was quiet I could sneak up to my room without Patch or Feb hearing me—if they were even home. But as the door squeaked in on its hinges, Feb and Patch were standing right inside. And they did *not* look too happy to see me.

"You are beyond grounded," Feb said, folding her arms.

I let the door slam shut behind me. After my whirlwind evening, this was so not what I needed, especially from my siblings. About a million times in the past, I'd come home the morning after a sleepover to find the house completely deserted; Patch would roll in an hour later, flop down on the couch, and fall asleep halfway through a DVD of *The Sopranos,* and Feb might not come home at all. I'd never complained, though—I was glad they had their own cool lives. Now they were mad because I'd stayed out past midnight?

"Where have you been?" Feb demanded. "We were worried sick."

"None of your business," I told her, scooping up Noodles. I glanced over at Patch, but he just stared at the floor. "If you guys were so worried, why didn't you just call my cell?"

"We did. I left you two voice mails."

"Oh. It must've been ringing when I left my purse in the club." Damn, damn, damn. Why couldn't I keep my big mouth shut? Noodles squirmed in my arms and whimpered. I set him down, and he ran away at top speed.

"After I told you no clubs?" Feb looked a little bit hurt, but she quickly snapped back to full-on anger mode. "I can't believe how irresponsible you're being!"

"Me, irresponsible? What planet are you living on? Patch, tell her she's insane!"

Patch studied his fingernails and mumbled, "I don't know, Flan. I think you should listen to your sister."

I looked at him speechlessly for moment, and then ran past them, up the stairs to my bedroom, where I slammed the door and flipped on the TV. I turned the volume way up, so Feb would be sure to hear it downstairs, before I turned it off again and thunked down in front of my desk. I switched on my laptop and opened up my instant messenger, but none of my friends were online. I was just about to check my e-mail when I heard someone tapping at my door.

"Flan?" It was Patch. I glared at him. He came in

and sat down on this pink suede beanbag chair I've had since forever. Patch isn't a little guy, and he looked pretty awkward sitting on it. It was hard to keep scowling at him, but I was still really mad.

"What is it?" I asked. "Did you come up here to confiscate my remote control?"

He looked embarrassed. "Nah, nothing like that."

"So . . . ?"

"I just think you should listen to Feb, Flan. I mean . . ." The bag crunched beneath him as he struggled to find the right words. "Look, it's just, she's never really cared this much about anybody before. You've given her, like, a purpose. We've got to support her, even if right now it seems like she's screwing up your life. You know what I mean?"

"No, Patch, I don't." Suddenly I just wanted him out of my room. I remembered the time in fifth grade, during my elephant phase, when he got back from one of his weeklong adventures and gave me a tiny silver elephant with jeweled eyes and a hooked trunk that I could keep my rings on. And I asked him where he got it and he couldn't remember. But that Patch felt a million miles away. "That makes no sense at all. My life is not just some *project* for Feb. It's *my life*." I turned back toward my computer. "Do me a favor, okay? Leave me alone. I don't want to talk about this anymore."

"Okay." I heard him get up and leave, but I didn't turn around until I heard the door click shut behind him. It was so weird—Patch is so laid-back and agreeable that I'd never really gotten mad at him before, but right then I was almost angrier at him than at Feb. How could he just sit back and let her do this to me?

I clicked on my new-mail folder. I had a ton of stuff: some spam, but mostly real e-mail, for a change. I clicked on the one from Bennett first.

> Subject: Lousy bf, worse writer
> Dear Flan,
> Sorry I had to leave right after the game tonight—that stupid article took me forever. Anyway, I wish I could've hung out with you longer, but hopefully you still had an okay time at the party with the 'diths.
> While I was writing, I was also listening to this new band, the Spectacles. I liked this song, and I thought you might too.
> —B.

He ended the article with a link to their MySpace page. I clicked on it, feeling guiltier than the time I broke my mom's favorite blown-glass vase and blamed it on my old friend Olivia. Bennett was so sweet, so smart, so sensitive. What on earth was wrong with me? I wished I'd never gone to that party.

The music was some sort of ambient rock with whooshing noises in the background—I preferred Leland Brinker's acoustic rock, but I made myself listen to it, and by the end I understood why he liked it so much. There was something kind of melancholy about the way the drums came in at the end. Closing the browser window, I thought about Bennett, his cute smile, his great sense of humor. I remembered holding hands with him at the football game and I started to feel more confused than ever.

I also had e-mails from Meredith and Judith. Bracing myself, I opened the one from Judith first.

> Subject: i'm so in loooove
>
> hey flan, so meredith was being annoying all the way back home but the thing is i just know that adam is meant 4 me!!!! you probably didn't even notice but he totally looked right up toward where we were sitting after he scored his touchdown and i think it meant that he loves me so i'm totally going after him. . . . i know i said i wouldn't but it's just like romeo and juliet and how would things have turned out 4 them if they hadn't started going out???

and meredith says i don't read. lol. anyway i
hope you're on my side in all this b/c i know
she's going to try to make you feel sorry for
her when adam and i are homecoming king
and queen!! lol. the thing is i really don't want
to hurt anyone but it's not my fault we belong
together. call me!!!! xoxo, j

ps kelvin just e-mailed me. how creepy is
that???

I sighed and opened the e-mail from Meredith.

Subject: floating in a dream
Oh, Flan! When I came home, I felt so
inspired! I wrote eight poems, made a collage,
and started knitting Adam a sweater. (I hope he
likes orange!) As you can probably tell, I'm in
love! There's no use denying it anymore! Why
live a life of self-sacrifice when "the birthday of
my life is come, my love is come to me"? As
soon as I finish the sweater, I'm going to tell him
how I feel! Or maybe I should write him a letter?
Meredith

I got up, drew the blinds, and changed into my
favorite cotton pajamas with the penguins on them.

Then I folded my Stuy tank top and took my new Betsey Johnson dress off my bed and hung it up in my closet. But before I shut the door, I stood there for a second looking at it. When I thought about how I'd been treating my friends—and Bennett—I felt like I never deserved to wear something so pretty ever again. I put on my fluffy slippers and consoled myself, thinking that at least it was all over for today. But when I sat back down to turn off the computer, there was a new message that had just come through, from an e-mail address I didn't recognize.

Subject: nice seeing you tonite
i hope you don't mind me e-mailing you, but i found your address on the bio homework site, so i thought i'd say hi. also, this picture cracked me up & i thought you might get a kick out of it. maybe this little guy was one of Bogie's pals back at the swamp!
adam

For a second, I started to feel terrible again—this problem with Adam just wasn't going to go away. Then I opened the picture and immediately started laughing. It was a purple salamander with a snail balanced on its head like a little hat. What made it so adorable was the expression on the salamander's face—it almost looked like it was smiling. I hit reply and typed something about how cute it was, but as I went to hit send, I realized what I was doing and canceled the message.

A couple days ago Adam had been barely a blip on my radar screen—if anything he was just one more lumbering jock to swerve past in the hallway on the way to class. But now he'd become this bizarre character who'd leapt unwanted out of Meredith and Judith's overblown romantic daydreams and into my own thoughts. He was like one of those annoying, poppy songs that make you groan when they come on the radio, but then somehow get stuck in your head. You find yourself humming them at the most random possible moments, like when you're standing in line at a deli and all of a sudden you realize that it's your turn in line but you still don't know what you want because you've been humming Shakira's "Hips Don't Lie" the entire time. And now he had kissed me.

I took one last look at the salamander, shut down my computer, and flipped off the lights. No more flirting with Adam, I told myself firmly as I curled up under the covers. I rested my head on my squishy down pillow and thought about the awful day I'd just had. My science teacher was going to make me murder Bogie,

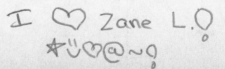

my friends were fighting over a guy, my sister had lost her mind, and I'd basically betrayed my boyfriend with someone I barely even knew. I knew things had gotten out of control when Sara-Beth Benny was the sanest person in my life. If things kept up like this, I'd have to move into my own bio-pod—no boys, friends, or siblings allowed.

Chapter 20

The next morning when I woke up, I yawned, stretched, and put my slippers on before I remembered I was "grounded." I figured I could do one of three things: sit in my room all day, have a big confrontation with Feb, or sneak out without her seeing me. There was no way I was going to do option number one, but another big fight didn't sound so great either. My throat was still sore from yelling at her—and at the game—the night before. So I put on my silver Tretorns and opted for choice number three.

A few years ago, in a rare moment of parental concern, my dad got a bunch of nylon ladders so, in case of emergency, we could climb out the second-story windows. I still had mine way in the back of my closet, under a bunch of old stuffed animals and feather boas I hadn't played with in years. I pulled it out, hooked the ends to the metal rail around my little balcony, and climbed down into the yard. I was a little nervous, especially because I had to climb past the kitchen windows on the first floor, but no one was looking out and I managed to get down into the yard okay. From there it was just a question of hoisting myself over the little wall between SBB's backyard and mine, which took about two seconds. As I jumped down from the wall, I felt really pleased with myself—until my sneakers hit a patch of gooey mud.

"Ugh!" I tried to kick the dirty splatters off the cuffs of my jeans. Despite all the interior-decoration chaos, Sara-Beth hadn't bothered to have her yard landscaped yet. Leaving a set of muddy footprints in my wake, I went up the stairs to her back door and knocked.

I had to wait almost fifteen minutes before Sara-Beth finally stopped sneaking around and peeking out the windows long enough to actually unlock the door.

"Thank God it's really you," she whispered, letting me inside. She immediately closed and locked the door behind me. "I was worried they sent a stalker in a Flan disguise!"

"Sorry I scared you," I said, pulling off my dirty sneakers. "I would've gone to your front door, but I'm supposed to be grounded."

I did a double take as Sara-Beth led me through the

kitchen and dining room toward the front of her house. The rugs, the furniture, even those famous silk curtains, had vanished. I checked my watch—hadn't I been in rococo France just a few hours ago? Noticing my reaction, Sara-Beth explained, "Oh, it was too old-fashioned. Now tell me what happened."

"There's not too much to tell." I sat down on the now-bare floor. "Feb's just acting like the overprotective mom I've never had—or wanted. It's really annoying."

"I hate to sound like a broken record, but I'll say it again: divorce her. Now, my lawyer—"

"I seriously don't think I can divorce my sister." I yawned. "Although the idea's sounding better all the time."

"Just let me know if you change your mind." Sara-Beth disappeared into the hallway for a minute and came back holding her cell phone. "Are you hungry? They took the refrigerator along with the rest of the furniture, but we can order in."

"They took the refrigerator? Why?"

"Well, actually it was a vintage icebox from Portugal and it barely worked anyway. I couldn't even find the power cord! Such a waste of money—oh, don't even get me started on Yvette." Sara-Beth dialed. "Hello? Is this Tavern on the Green? This is

Sara-Beth Benny. I was just wondering if you deliver. What?! Do you even know who I am?"

Half an hour later, we were eating brioche French toast and drinking fresh-squeezed orange juice out of paper containers on SBB's floor.

"Decorating this place has been such a nightmare," she moaned, cutting her French toast into miniscule squares. "I just want to give up. These incompetent designers take advantage of me at every turn."

"I think you just have to figure out what you really want, you know?" I said around a mouthful of maple syrup and blueberries. It was a little soggy. "It seems like everybody else has been forcing their taste on you. But it's your house."

"Wow! That's exactly right, Flan. It's like when I was growing up. They told me how to dress, what to say, where to stand—it was like I was some kind of puppet."

"Well, you were acting in a TV show," I pointed out. "There was a script. And a director."

"That's no excuse!" Sara-Beth frowned as she took a sip of her orange juice. Then she brightened up again. "Flan, I've got an idea."

"What?"

"It's almost Halloween. I should decorate this place

like a haunted house! Just until I can think of how I really want it to look, you know. And then we can throw a costume party and it'll take your mind off your troubles and—oh, it's a perfect idea!"

I nodded slowly. I wasn't sure I deserved a party after the way I'd been acting, but Meredith and Judith did love Halloween. Maybe it would be a nice way to start healing our friendship. We could get all dressed up together beforehand, and then maybe sleep over at my house.

"So, who should we invite?" I asked, really warming to the idea.

"All the best people, of course! We can invite February, and your brother, of course, so they can't possibly object to you coming. And oh, Haley Joel, I owe him an invitation—we can even call Ashleigh-Ann Martin! It'll be a fresh new start for all of us!" Sara-Beth laughed merrily, then turned serious. "But everyone has to wear a costume. Absolutely no exceptions." Her eyes widened. "Once I was the only one in costume at a party in Beverly Hills, and I've never gotten over the humiliation."

"Why? What were you dressed up as?"

"Not important." Sara-Beth shook the frown off face and clapped in excitement. "Flan, this is going to be the best party of all time. I can hardly wait!"

"Me neither," I said. But somewhere in the back of my mind, I was still worried. The last party I'd been to had ended in disaster—what if something even worse happened this time? But I so wanted to go for it. After all, I love Halloween. . . .

Chapter 21

I still didn't want to deal with Patch and Feb, so after I left SBB's house I called Meredith and Judith to invite them out for coffee. I hesitated for a second, feeling guilty, then called Bennett, too.

"Hey, what's up?" he asked. "I was worried you were mad at me or something."

"Why would I be mad at you?" Great—I'd been talking to Bennett for all of three seconds and I was already feeling even more terrible about myself than I had before. I started walking toward the Bean Garden. "*You're* perfect."

"But I took off so early last night, and then you didn't write back to me. You know, about that band."

"Oh yeah, the Spectacles. I'm sorry." I stopped to look at my reflection in the window of a MAC store. I wondered how long it would be before he found out what a terrible girlfriend I really was. "I was kind of . . . distracted last night. I got into a fight with Feb."

"She's still a desperate housewife?"

I sighed. "Serial mom's more like it." I started walking again. "Hey, do you have any plans for Halloween yet? Because Sara-Beth's throwing a haunted-house party."

"Man, I wish I could be there, but I promised I'd take my cousin trick-or-treating."

"Really? That's so sweet. But can't you just come by after?"

"Well, uh, I think my parents want me to babysit." Bennett's voice sounded a little funny. I narrowed my eyes. Was he lying to me?

"How old's your cousin?"

"Ummm . . . eight?" It sounded like a question.

Hmm. "That's . . . nice." I was in front of the Bean Garden by now. "Listen, I'm going to get some coffee with Judith and Meredith. Come meet us."

"Nah, that's okay. I'm right in the middle of alpha-betizing my comic book collection by illustrator, and if I leave them all over the living room floor my mom'll kill me." I heard pages rustling in the background. "Hey, by the way, how was the party last night? You tell Adam I said congrats?"

Blood rushed into my face, and I coughed to hide

the awkward pause. "Yeah—no. I mean, I didn't really get a chance to talk to him."

Meredith and Judith showed up about fifteen minutes later, looking like they'd bickered the whole way over on the subway. I had wanted to surprise them with news about the party, but SBB had already sent them Evites.

"This party is going to be the event of the semester," Judith declared with obvious satisfaction. A terrible thought crossed my mind.

"What do you mean, 'the event of the semester'?" I asked.

"I mean, just because SBB always throws the best parties," Judith clarified lamely.

Meredith giggled loudly for a second too long. "Let's go shopping for costumes! Right now!" She was wearing a bunch of beaded necklaces I'd never seen before. I wondered if they were part of her explosion of creativity from the night before, but I didn't dare ask.

The three of us walked over to Screaming Mimi's on Lafayette Street, a little store that sells vintage costumes, and we started hunting through the clothing racks. I was mostly looking at classic things like old flapper dresses with seed-bead stitching, puffy crinolines, and a suede cowgirl suit from the '40s, but

Meredith and Judith went straight for all the more . . . *alluring* things in the store: a skintight catsuit, a super-short white mod dress with matching thigh-high go-go boots, a '50s-style yellow bikini top with Daisy Dukes. But when none of these fit quite right, they insisted we shop somewhere more "modern." So I put the feath-ered, antique Mardi Gras mask I was holding back on the shelf, and we piled into a cab to go a little farther uptown to Ricky's NYC, a big costume superstore.

This place had plenty of variations on the sexy bunny/policewoman/nurse–type getups, and Meredith and Judith ran around like crazy, dodging little kids waving plastic swords, exhausted-looking parents with baby bags on their shoulders, and display rack after display rack of brightly colored costumes in square plastic bags. While Meredith was in the dressing room trying on a very revealing ladybug ensemble, Judith snuck up behind me and tapped my shoulder.

"Flan," she whispered, "I'm so excited about this party. You know why?"

Actually, I didn't really want to know, but it seemed like I didn't have much choice. "Why?"

"Because I'm going to invite Adam! When I was Googling him last night, I found his e-mail address, and I'm going to send the invitation to him as soon as I get home." She flipped her hair. "I just have to find an amazing costume first. There's no point inviting him if I'm not the hottest one there!"

My heart sank. "Judith, please, please don't do this," I begged. "You promised you'd leave him alone. Remember your promise?"

Judith picked up a low-cut stewardess costume and held it at arm's length, considering it. "Listen, if I don't do it, Meredith will. You saw the way she was giggling earlier."

"How can you say that about your best friend? I mean, don't you trust her at all?"

Just then Meredith skipped out of the dressing room, wearing a red-and-black leotard, fishnets, and red patent leather pumps with three-inch heels. A head-band with glittery red-and-black antennae bobbled on her head. She struck a pose. "So . . . how do I look?"

Judith glanced over at me significantly, like she was trying to say, *See, I told you so!* I sighed, realizing she was probably right, but I didn't want to be in the middle or take sides, so I just stared back at her like I had no idea what she meant.

Judith found a costume that rivaled Meredith's on the scandalous-scale: a pirate getup with a striped bandana and cutlass. Her patent-leather high-heeled boots almost reached her knees, but her frayed black skirt ended way, way above them. It took me a lot longer to find my costume, but when I did I was glad I'd taken my time. It was a powder blue princess dress, a little bit like Cinderella's, with puffy sleeves and this really delicate silver stitching on the skirt. Even though it was a little expensive, I knew the minute I saw it that I had to have it. I decided to wear it with my pair of clear Lucite heels I'd bought for a dance way back in seventh grade, just to complete the Cinderella look. I was really excited. This is why I love Halloween: it's like my last chance to play dress-up the way I did when I was younger. I could tell Meredith and Judith thought my costume was kind of lame, but they didn't say anything. I got the feeling they were a little relieved I wasn't going to outshine them by wearing something even more revealing than they were. Although I wasn't really sure that was possible. After we paid, their shopping bags were so tiny, it looked like they'd gone shopping for handkerchiefs—which in a way, I guess they had.

We stepped outside, but all of a sudden Judith realized she'd left her hair clip back in the dressing room and went racing inside to get it. The minute she was out of sight, Meredith leaned in toward me and, glancing back and forth to make sure no one was watching, whispered, "Flan, I hope you won't be mad at me, but I wanted to ask you something."

I sighed. "Shoot."

"Would you hate me if I invited Adam to the party? I was going to do it before—but then I thought maybe I should talk to you first. Please, please say you won't hate me." She looked at me with her large, pale eyes, and I found myself shaking my head. After what had happened between Adam and me, how could I possibly judge her for wanting to see him again? I was the biggest violator of the No Adam Rule—and they didn't even know it.

"Of course not," I told her. "I could never hate you for something like that. But are you sure it's the best idea? It's really Judith you should be asking, not me."

"She'd never understand, but it's just something I have to do." Meredith's eyes got sort of starry and far-away. "It just feels right."

To me, though, everything just felt wrong. Judith came out and the three of us continued down the street. As I carried my new dress along in its bag, I couldn't help but wish that something—anything—would keep Adam away from this party, because there was no way Meredith and Judith were going to be able to control themselves around him. Not that I blamed them—self-control around Adam wasn't exactly something I had lots of either.

I still held on to the hope that Judith and Meredith would be too shy to go through with inviting Adam to the party. One time, when she was first crushing on Jules, Meredith had actually jumped into a janitor's closet when she saw him coming toward her down the hall, because she was convinced that she had something stuck between her teeth. Judith liked to exude confidence, but if she sat next to Eric (or anybody else from her "Stuy Guy" top ten list) at a school assembly, she spent the entire time either staring straight ahead or furiously scribbling in her notebook.

But when I got to biology on Monday the first thing Adam said with that friendly smile of his was, "Meredith and Judith forwarded me the invite to your friend's Halloween party. I'll definitely be there."

Damn, damn, damn. "Oh . . . that's, uh, great."

I blinked once and tried to hide my rapidly cycling emotions of fear (how was this going to turn out?), guilt (why had I wanted him to kiss me?), and—all right, I'll admit it—excitement (I really needed to have my head examined). I really hoped Adam didn't think I'd put Meredith and Judith up to e-mailing him, but I didn't exactly know how to clarify the situation without making an already terrible situation even worse. I hung my schoolbag off the back of my chair and willed the blood to stop rushing to my face. Just seeing him again, after everything that had happened, was making me very confused.

"So, how do you know Sara-Beth Benny, anyway?" he asked.

There's a long story behind the first time Sara-Beth and I hung out, but it seemed best to spend as little time as possible talking to Adam, because every time I talked to him, I seemed to like him more, which could only lead to all around badness and complication. I stared past Adam to the poster of the periodic table on the opposite wall and said simply, "We're next-door neighbors."

"Wow. That's pretty amazing. You know, she gets a lot of crap in the tabloids, but she's actually a talented actress. I saw her in that remake of *Breathless* and was really impressed. And it seemed like a demanding role—she had to talk nonstop for practically the entire two-hour movie."

"Well, that's Sara-Beth for you." I said with a tiny smile, wishing I could tell him that nearly two more hours of SBB's endless monologue had ended up on the cutting room floor. I knew it was the right thing to do, but I felt guilty being so cold to him. Because the truth was, I liked that he'd seen *Breathless,* and that he thought SBB was a good actress. A lot of people don't know about her artsy stuff, and think she's just a huge party girl because she's always on the cover of *US Weekly*. And it wasn't his fault that Meredith and Judith were in love with him. Plus, I didn't want him to feel weird about The Kiss. I hadn't told him Bennett was my boyfriend, and I wasn't actually mad at him for kissing me. I was mad at myself for wanting him to.

Adam looked at me steadily with a questioning look in his soft green eyes, clearly a little confused at my unresponsiveness. "Anyhow, it's cool you're friends with her."

"She's a good friend," I said, pulling my lab notebook out of my schoolbag. "Okay. So, let's get started here."

Adam and I spent the first few minutes of class silently taking down our observations on Bogie—how big he was, if he was starting to develop arms, and how much his back legs had grown.

The silence got to me after five quiet minutes had passed. "Sorry if it seems like I'm in a bad mood today," I said, shaking some flakes of frog food onto the surface of the water. "I found out over the weekend what's going to happen to Bogie, and I guess it still really bothers me."

A tiny worry line appeared between his eyebrows. "What do you mean?"

"We're going to have to dissect him at the end of the unit."

"No way!" Adam looked at the frog with genuine concern. "That's totally ridiculous. I can't believe it."

I stared despondently at Bogie. He was getting cuter every day: his eyes were big and sweet and wet looking, and he was already starting to peek up above the surface of the water with this expression of total love, like he wanted to climb out on land just to be closer to us. And his fins were turning into little frog hands—webbed and suction-cuppy, but somehow kind of human too. Looking at him made me think about the frogs out by the pond at our summerhouse in Greenwich, Connecticut. When I was little, I used to go out early in the morning with a bowl of granola and eat while I watched them sit on their lily pads.

I believed their loud croaking was how they sang to one another. I knew there was no way I was going to hurt Bogie, even if it meant flunking a class.

"What're we going to do?" Adam reached into the jar to pat Bogie's slimy forehead with his little finger.

"I don't know. We could start a petition and give it to the principal, asking to release them."

"Yeah, but where would they go?" He glanced out the window at the tall buildings. "It's not exactly like we're out in the middle of nature."

I bit my lip. "Well, we have to do something!"

"Hey, don't worry. We'll come up with a plan." Adam squeezed my shoulder comfortingly. It was just a friendly thing to do, but it was the first time he'd touched me since The Kiss. My heart racing, I stared down at my lab notebook, not quite sure how to respond.

"So, what are you dressing up as?" I stammered, changing the subject.

"For Halloween? I hadn't really thought about it. I guess I wasn't really thinking that I'd wear a costume."

"Well, SBB's not letting anybody in who doesn't have a costume." I immediately wished I hadn't said anything. It would probably be way better for everybody if he got turned away at the door.

"For real?"

I shook my head, trying to undo some of the damage. "Oh, probably not. Sara-Beth always threatens crazy stuff like that and never does it. Actresses just like to be dramatic, you know?"

"Well, that's good. My costumes have always been kind of bad." He smiled, and his green eyes sparkled. I kicked myself for finding him so cute. "When I was a kid, I was a pirate for like five years in a row, and this was long before Johnny Depp made them hip."

I thought of Judith's pirate costume and felt a pang of jealousy. Maybe he would think she looked cuter than I did. Then I felt like smacking my forehead in disgust. What was wrong with me? It wasn't like Adam was my boyfriend—he shouldn't even be my crush. Hadn't I told myself a million times already that I was going to stop flirting with this guy? "Well, it must be fun for you to be on a team called the Peglegs."

"No kidding! Maybe I'll just stick on my jersey and helmet and 'pretend' to be a football player." Class was almost over; Adam started screwing the lid back on Bogie's jar. "What are you going as?"

"You'll just have to wait and see." I closed up my notebook and clicked my pen shut. "My friends think it's kind of silly, but I like it."

"I can't wait." The way he said it made my knees wobble a little. Was it possible he was going to this party just because of me? I hoped not—but at the same time, the thought made me a little giddy. As the bell rang, Adam picked up his backpack and swung it over his shoulder. I noticed that the little white bandage on his elbow was still there. "See you later, Flan."

"See ya." He loped off into the hallway, but I was slow to leave the classroom. I needed a minute to think.

Adam was wrong for me in every way. I knew that crushing on him could only mess up my life—but somehow when I looked into those eyes . . . Well, he was just so confident and sure of himself, like he knew exactly who he was and what he wanted. I wished I could be more like that. And when I was with him I had that crazy fitting-together feeling where everything was just . . . effortless. But if I ended up with Adam, than I was pretty sure nobody would talk to me for the rest of high school. So I shook off every thought of him—as much as that was even possible. . . .

I didn't really want to get in another huge fight with Feb, so instead of heading straight over to SBB's place after school, I went home to drop off my school-books and tell her where I was going. When I got inside the house, I found her sitting at the kitchen table, wearing an old chenille bathrobe of our mom's, drinking coffee and writing out an extensive to-do list. A pile of law briefs stamped CONFIDENTIAL sat next to her on the table.

"Flan, I noticed that you didn't make your bed this morning," she snapped as I walked past her toward the refrigerator. "I want this house to look cleaner."

"Did *you* make your bed this morning? Or even once when you were in high school?" I asked, pushing aside some sketchy-looking leftovers and reaching for the peach-mango juice.

"Be that as it may," she grumbled, tapping at her calculator. I rolled my eyes. "Hey—I saw that."

"Give it a rest, okay Feb?" I plopped down on a chair across from her. "I want my sister back."

"And I want you to learn some responsibility. Life isn't just an endless series of parties, Flan. It's hard work and . . . and a bunch of other stuff too."

I sighed and wished that I'd told Sara-Beth not to invite Feb to the Halloween party after all. She'd probably just spend the whole evening trying to get people to clean up after themselves and sign up for SAT prep classes and God knows what else.

"Listen, I'm going over to Sara-Beth's house for a while," I said, putting my juice glass in the sink. "I'll be home in time for dinner, okay?"

"Absolutely not! You're not going anywhere till I see your homework all finished and ready to turn in."

"I'll work on my homework over there!"

"You'll work on your homework upstairs in your own bedroom where you can concentrate."

"You've got to be kidding me." I stomped away.

"Learning responsibility is a good thing!" Feb called after me. "One day you'll thank me for this!"

"I seriously doubt that!"

I sighed, exhausted from all the sharp words. What the hell had happened to the girl who never left home without her cell-phone-shaped flask? Who never once said the word *homework* without rolling her eyes? Who got so wrapped up in her social life she forgot to come home for weeks on end? Who taught me how to swing dance in the middle of Central Park? I almost felt like crying as I slammed my door shut and locked it. My parents were off on some transcontinental voyage, my sister was an alien, and Patch was supporting her over me. Well, just because Feb had decided out of the blue that she was "responsible" didn't mean I had to follow suit. I got the rope ladder out of my closet and climbed down into the yard to visit Sara-Beth Benny.

When I got over to Sara-Beth's house, the back door was propped open with a toolbox. A half dozen men in splattered coveralls were painting the walls and ceiling while several others installed new cabinets in the kitchen. It was kind of incredible what they'd accomplished—the place seriously looked like something out of a horror film. The new cupboards all had big gashes and dents in them, like the murderer from *Texas Chainsaw Massacre* had moved to Manhattan and taken a dislike to the décor. The walls were now a dark, smoky gray and the trim was a rich, pumpkiny orange. The walls that had dried had delicate cobwebs stenciled onto them, and one painter was carefully flicking crimson droplets onto the floorboards. It took me a minute to understand what he was doing, but then I noticed Sara-Beth Benny lying nearby, her arms and legs splayed like she'd fallen from the ceiling. Someone had outlined her body in white, like the chalk outlines they do around corpses at crime scenes, and "blood" splatters fanned out from her bent body.

"Flan, I'm so glad to see you!" Sara-Beth grinned up at me from her dead-body position on the floor. She was wearing a lacy black top and a necklace strung with little spider charms. "What do you think? Isn't it spectacular?"

"It's fantastic!" And I meant it—there was something eerie about this particular style and how it really did seem to match the house well. Or maybe it just matched Sara-Beth. . . .

"Have you met my new designer? Lenore? Lenoore!" Sara-Beth called. A woman with long dark hair and a flowing burgundy velvet skirt bustled into the room. She wore a black corset that was so tight it looked like it was cracking her ribs, and her arms were almost as skeletal as Sara-Beth's.

"I just got off the phone with the taxidermist." Lenore clasped her hands together and smiled with pure delight. "He said the ravens and black cats should be ready by tomorrow morning. And if you still want the two-headed rabbit, he has one in stock."

"Oh, absolutely. But it must be pure white with big shiny red eyes! Isn't that wonderful, Flan?" Sara-Beth asked, her eyes shining. "The animals are going to be beautiful. He's won all kinds of awards."

"That's . . . great," I said, wondering what kind of awards a taxidermist could win.

"Now, if you'll excuse me, I still have to call Evolution about getting those skeletons delivered." Lenore smiled at me pleasantly. Her eyeteeth were exceptionally pointy. "Nice meeting you."

"I'm so excited about this party," said SBB, getting up carefully to avoid smudging her outline on the floor. "Have you picked out a costume yet?"

"Actually, I have. I'm going to be a princess," I said. "Do you think that's stupid?"

"Not at all! Oh, you always come up with the cutest ideas. In fact . . ." Sara-Beth snapped her fingers. "I'll be right back."

She left me standing there awkwardly with the workmen while she disappeared up the stairs. I looked around for somewhere to sit down before I remembered she'd gotten rid of all her furniture. Fortunately, Sara-Beth is almost as quick as she is tiny, and she came back in no time at all.

"Someone gave this to me eons ago—I wore it in a cereal commercial where I played a princess who wouldn't eat anything but Double Fluff Rice Sugar Puff Flakes," she explained, holding out a box. "I still remember my line: 'But Daddy, I won't eat anything but my Double Fluff Rice Sugar Puff Flakes!'" She laughed. "Take it from me, once we actors really get into a character, they're always there, inside of us. I can't even tell you how many voices I'm hearing in my head right now! But, anyway, you can have this, because it's just totally going to waste."

I opened the box and gasped. Inside was the prettiest, most elaborate silver crown I'd ever seen. It had little jewels in it, and this sort of delicate filigree that made it sparkle under the light. I took it out of the case and put it on my head. It fit perfectly.

"You look adorable!" Sara-Beth clapped her hands. "I don't know how I'm going to sleep tonight, I'm so excited. Can you believe Halloween is tomorrow?"

I put the crown back into its case. "If I'm even allowed to go," I said gloomily. "Did you already send the Evite to Feb and Patch?"

"Oh no! I forgot!" Sara-Beth pulled out her BlackBerry and started pushing buttons frantically. I snatched it out of her hands.

"Wait! I'm glad you didn't. Feb's acting like such a controlling mother, I'd rather not have her at the party staring over my shoulder and judging everything I do."

I shook the image of Feb chasing me around SBB's party with a spatula out of my head and handed the BlackBerry back. "I'll just tell her I'm coming over here to watch movies, and by the time she figures out what's happening, it'll be too late for her to do anything about it."

"All right," Sara-Beth agreed, inspecting a new cobweb on the wall. "Are your friends still coming?"

"Well, Bennett can't make it, but Meredith and Judith are going to be here. And unfortunately, they invited Adam too."

"Unfortunately? Flan, you're so silly!" Sara-Beth tiptoed through the splatters of "blood" on her floor. "I can't wait to meet him. Why wouldn't you want him to be here?"

"I don't know, it's just so confusing." I hugged the crown box and looked down at my shoes. "Meredith and Judith are going to be clawing each other's eyes out. . . . I guess the truth is, I wish I didn't like him so much."

"Ah, young love." Sara-Beth sighed, adjusting the spider charms on her necklace. I didn't bother reminding her she was only three years older than me. "Maybe since you're dressing up as a princess with my bee-yoo-tiful tiara, he'll come dressed as a prince and ride in on a horse, like Liesel did for her sweet sixteen, and then he'll swoop you up and kiss you at midnight—oh my God, can you picture anything more romantic—and then it'll really be like a fairy tale. . . ."

SBB rhapsodized for several more minutes about my budding fairy-tale romance with Adam, but no matter how hard I tried, I kept getting stuck on the midnight kiss part.

Chapter 24

*T*he next day was Halloween, and the whole school day was one big celebration. It was like Halloween madness had taken the place of football fever: all the teachers were giving away Snickers bars and bags of Skittles, and one peppy cheerleader type was even handing out pirate-shaped cookies that you could color in yourself, like those ones you can buy at Mets games. By the middle of the day everyone was way too sugared-up and hyper to get any real work done. Even though it was all kind of silly and over the top, it was nice, too, because with all the cheesy orange crepe paper decorations and the geeky math teachers in Harry Potter hats and the iPod speakers playing "The Monster Mash" in the halls, I almost forgot to worry about the party that night.

After school, Judith and Meredith came back to my neighborhood with me to get dressed up in our costumes and watch the Halloween parade. I was glad when we walked into my house that Feb was nowhere in sight—it would have been really embarrassing if she lectured my friends on their scanty costumes or did something else equally horrifying. We played with Noodles for a while—he always does this insanely cute thing where he stands up on his hind legs and tries to kiss my friends right on the lips—and then we snacked on whatever we could find, which was hummus and pita bread and carrot sticks and cheese. As I munched on a piece of slightly hard Wisconsin cheddar, I found myself wishing that if I had to put up with Feb's psycho mom routine, she had at least kept up the cookie-making phase a little bit longer.

After we finished eating, we went up to my room to get dressed and put on all our makeup. Even though her ladybug costume wasn't the most creative, Meredith managed to do some really artistic things with her makeup—she put on red glitter eye shadow that gave her a great, devilish quality, and she put a couple of black dots high on each cheek. I had her do my makeup, too, but Judith wouldn't let Meredith get near her with the eyebrow pencil—it was obvious she thought Meredith was planning to sabotage with a fake mustache or something, which struck me as a little paranoid.

"Okay, I admit I had my doubts," Judith told me once she saw me in costume. "But you look gorgeous. Where'd you get that crown?"

"Beauty contest." The two of them looked at me all surprised. "Kidding. Sara-Beth gave it to me."

I gave myself one last look-over in the mirror. Maybe I hadn't put on a sexy pirate dress or a ladybug leotard like my friends, but I thought I looked really nice. I felt sad that Bennett wouldn't get to see my costume, and then felt guilty because I hoped Adam would think I looked pretty.

"What's wrong?" Meredith asked, tilting her head at my reflection in the mirror.

I shook my head quickly. "Nothing. Come on, let's go." I put on my clear Lucite shoes and grabbed my purse, and the three of us hurried out to watch the parade. It didn't start for another hour, but we wanted to get a good spot, and some people camped out there hours ahead of time.

The Halloween parade is just about the wildest thing I've ever seen in Manhattan. It turns my neighborhood into a complete zoo every year—literally about two million people show up for it—but I don't mind, because it's like Mardi Gras, the Macy's Thanksgiving Day parade, and an avant-garde performance-art piece all rolled into one. Every year it starts out with the puppets, these enormous living sculptures that go flailing down the street, in front of all the floats and stuff. Skeleton-shaped puppets usually go first, and I've also seen puppets of the Statue of Liberty, robots, monkeys, and Godzilla. They used to give me nightmares when I was a kid—some of them move so realistically they almost look like they're alive—or dead—but now I'm so used to seeing them that it wouldn't feel like Halloween without them.

It's also worth going to the parade just to see everybody's costumes. Anyone is allowed to join the Halloween parade, and a lot of people from my neighborhood get really into dressing up for it. I've never done it, but plenty of times I've seen Patch and his buddies go marching by dressed as gladiators or ninjas or whatever else they think is cool that year. Other people dress up in way weirder costumes, though. A lot of people go in pairs—ketchup and mustard, a policeman and a doughnut; once I even saw three people dressed up as rock, paper, and scissors, which I thought was pretty cute. And I'll never forget the year I saw a big burly guy dressed as Cruella de Vil chasing about twenty people in Dalmatian suits around the corner onto Perry Street.

Anyway, the parade is usually a blast, and this year was no exception. Meredith and Judith and I stood there on the sidewalk for about an hour, laughing and clapping and cheering at all the wild stuff going by, and I never got tired of it, not even when some kid dropped his ice cream right next to my shoes and started screaming at the top of his lungs and his mother (who was dressed as a pumpkin) had to elbow past us to get him out of the crowd. Nor did I mind the guy who stood two feet away playing a tuneless song on the accordion, because his tinfoil trench coat was actually kind of cool.

After a while, though, we decided it was time to go to the party—my Lucite shoes were cute but not that comfortable to stand in, and Meredith and Judith seemed awfully anxious to get over to Sara-Beth's before a certain somebody arrived. We tried to push back through the crunch toward Perry Street, but it was practically impossible with all of the fake Siamese twins and Medusas pressing in on all sides. Judith and I lost Meredith for a second, and we almost panicked, but then we caught a glimpse of her four feet away, hanging on to a lamppost as the Seven Dwarves and a flock of evil stepmothers swarmed around her. After what seemed like forever, the three of us finally broke free from the crowd and, brushing off the fairy dust an overeager Tinkerbell had just sprinkled on us, we walked back through my neighborhood toward the party.

"That was a really beautiful parade," I said. "It was so great how they got those cannons on the Captain Hook ship to fire candy out into the crowd."

"I loved that float with all the people dressed as body parts." Meredith laughed. "I've never seen a gallbladder before, but I bet that's exactly what they look like."

"Ugh—that float was so gross. And I'm quite sure it was inaccurate." Judith shot Meredith a smug, sidelong glance, like she really wanted to say, *But that's okay, because a weirdo like you could never steal my future boyfriend.* Then she said sweetly, "Meredith, I think your makeup's getting a little smudged. You're looking less 'ladybug' and more 'drippy insect bug.' You should probably get some fresh eyeliner.'"

"Omigod!" Meredith's hands flew to her face, and she raced to the pharmacy at the next corner. Judith and I waited outside for her, watching as a witch and a fluffy red bird walked past.

"I thought her makeup looked okay," I said to Judith, trying to keep the conversation neutral. I was worried she would try to bring up Adam, and I just couldn't stand to hear about him right then. I felt so nervous about the evening: one part of me was feeling sick to my stomach at the thought of seeing him again; another part of me was worried about my friends seeing him; and the last part of me—the worst part of me—was already practically bursting with excitement.

"Whatever. I just wanted a chance to talk to you alone." Judith glanced back and forth surreptitiously, then whispered, "I'm sure I'm going to kiss Adam tonight. My parents always tell me you can get anything you set your mind to, and it's true. I've thought everything about this all the way through and I'm not taking no for an answer."

"Oh, Judith, just . . . don't do something you'll regret." My heart twisted in my chest; why did this have to be happening?

She laughed and flipped her hair. "Believe me, I won't."

"All done," Meredith sang as she skipped toward us with a little plastic bag. "One of my glitter eyelashes was drooping a little. And I found this amazing red glitter lipstick—isn't it perfect?" She stuck the lipstick in her purse and we walked on toward Perry Street.

Judith strode ahead of us like she wanted to be first in the room to pick her seat for the PSAT, while Meredith and I lagged behind. Meredith was busy delighting in every new sight and sound, and I was having trouble keeping up, because my Lucite heels were absolutely killing my feet. Even though I was wearing my Cinderella dress, I felt suspiciously like one of her ugly stepsisters—apparently I'd gone up a shoe size since I'd bought these two years earlier.

"Isn't Halloween great?" asked Meredith, admiring some pumpkins wearing sunglasses in the window of an eyeglass shop. "I think it's my favorite holiday."

"Yeah, it's cool I guess," I said warily, aware of where this conversation could go.

"And it's such a beautiful night!" Meredith sniffed the air. "I just feel, like . . . currents of energy—really good energy." She smiled contentedly and lowered her voice. "It's going to happen with Adam tonight, I just know it. I feel like it's meant to be."

I looked down at my feet, which were starting to blister. "Well, I'm glad you're so happy. But are you sure this is what you really want? There'll be some major consequences—*best friend* consequences—if something does happen."

Meredith took a deep breath. "I just hope he shows up. Then everything will be perfect. It might take her a little while, but Judith will understand. Besides, I know *you'll* be my friend no matter what happens."

I bit my lip and said nothing. If Adam did come to the party, it didn't seem like things could turn out perfectly for any of us. Even though that terrible part of me wanted to see Adam tonight, for the first time I really truly hoped he wouldn't show up. Because as we went up the steps to Sara-Beth's town house, I had a feeling—as strong as Meredith and Judith's feeling that tonight was their night to win Adam—that tonight would be the night when something terrible, maybe even irreversible, would happen to our friendship.

When we stepped inside Sara-Beth Benny's newly haunted house, the party had most definitely begun. It was like the entire Halloween parade had migrated into her living room. Jack Sparrow and the Zodiac were arguing with each other across a cauldron filled with punch; the Bride from *Kill Bill* was hitting on Frankenstein; Spider-Man was eating a cookie shaped like a broomstick. "Thriller" blasted at top volume from speakers camouflaged as furry black bats up in the corners of the room, and in the spaces where there wasn't a crush of bodies, I could see that SBB's new furniture had arrived: strewn around the room were a dingy, molding Victorian-era sofa, an electric chair (unplugged, I hoped), and a bench made out of what looked like a coffin on stilts.

I couldn't believe how many people had shown up. I had thought Sara-Beth was inviting twenty or so at most.

But now her town house was stuffed so full of monsters and superheroes I could barely make my way across the room. Most of the people looked like they were from Stuyvesant—how many people had Judith and Meredith invited?—but with all the elaborate costumes I couldn't be sure. One thing I did notice, though, was the unusual number of Kermit-the-frogs wandering around. They all had on these terrycloth suits that looked like little kids' footie pajamas, and big plastic masks like mascot heads that covered their entire faces. They were cute, sure, but there were an awful lot of them.

"I'm going to look for Sara-Beth," I yelled to Meredith and Judith over the blasting music, then pushed on through the crowd. The fact was, I needed to get away from the two of them for a while. Watching them scan the room for Adam made me feel guilty and nervous—and a little bit giddy too.

Almost as soon as I got away from Judith and Meredith, I spotted Liesel—the Ice Queen herself. Seriously. She was dressed in a powder blue Carolina Herrera gown, with white glitter accents around her eyes, and an icicle-like clear plastic chopstick speared through her done-up hair.

"Darling, you look adorable!" She flung her arms around me and we air-kissed. "How long have you been here?"

"I just got here. But I thought you were going to be at the Museum of Modern Art tonight. Don't you have a benefit gala or something?"

Liesel waved away the question. "They'll get along all right without me. When I found out about this, I knew I couldn't miss it. The last time Sara-Beth threw a party, I woke up the next morning with a new PR project and Ashton Kutcher's number in my phone!" She looked over my shoulder. "Although the crowd here does seem a little younger this time . . ."

"Well, I better find Sara-Beth. Have you seen her?"

"She's upstairs. Bye-bye, snookums! Kisses!"

Waving to Liesel, I pushed past two Kermits, a Batman, a Hermione, and some girl in a bubble-wrap dress as I went up the stairs. Considering how crazy the place was, Sara-Beth Benny was surprisingly easy to find. She was in her upstairs den, working the room with a bowl of cold pasta.

"Feel these brains!" she was shouting to a confused-looking Oompa-Loompa. "Aren't they disgusting? But it's really cold spaghetti! Touch it anyway! Cold spaghetti!" Then she spotted me and gasped with delight, almost dropping the spaghetti brains on the blood-splattered floor. "Flan, you look adorable!"

"Thanks. You do too." I wasn't really sure who Sara-Beth was supposed to be; she had on the tight, lacy black dress and dark red tulle train that she'd bought with me earlier that week, but she hadn't done anything to make her costume more specific. She could have been dressed as a vampire, an undead prom queen, or as herself at an awards ceremony. It wasn't until she shoved the bowl of pasta at me and grabbed her pointy black hat off a chair that I figured out she was supposed to be a witch. "This place is packed," I added, glancing around. "I had no idea you invited so many people."

"Oh, I didn't. But news about these things spreads like some kind of disease!" Sara-Beth shook her head. "Not that I blame anyone. If I got invited to a party like this, I'd tell everyone too."

"So the invite got out?" I looked around, shaking my head. No wonder all of Stuyvesant seemed to be here. "That's terrible!"

"My only concern is the paparazzi, of course, but they'll never recognize me like this!" She stuck her hand into the bowl spaghetti she'd made me hold and wiggled it around with horrified delight. "Eww! It feels so weird. You can carry it around for a while. People love it! Cold spaghetti!"

"I think you're actually supposed to pass it around in a dark room," I explained. "When people can't see what it is, they think that it's brains."

Sara-Beth ignored me.

"Now," she said, linking her arm through mine, "you're going to have to point out this Adam character to me. I need to see the boy who's causing my sweet Flan so much trouble!"

"I don't think he's here yet," I said, setting the pasta bowl down on top of a large steel cage we passed. Inside, a large black cobra stared up at me, motionless. I decided to believe it was stuffed.

On the way down the stairs, we passed a guy whom I vaguely recognized from my algebra class. He was wearing jeans and a T-shirt.

"Oh, no, you don't!" Sara-Beth stopped on the stairs and wagged a finger at him. "No costume, no party."

The guy glanced sheepishly from her to me to her again, to see if she was joking. She wasn't.

"I really was going to get one," he explained, "but I didn't get a chance this afternoon."

"No excuses! Go straight down to the basement. Thorn will take care of you there." Then she pulled out a little cell phone, punched a number, and said, "Thorn? One medium size guy, on his way down."

"Thorn?" The guy gulped. Sara-Beth stared at him mercilessly, her bony arms crossed, and he backed down the stairs.

"He better actually go to the basement," she said. "If I see him in here again like that, I'm sending Thorn up here to get him."

"You're really serious about this costume rule," I observed. "What's in the basement?"

"All kinds of medieval torture thingies. But most of those are just for show. I sent that boy there to get his costume. A friend of Lenore's at Halloween Adventure sold us a surplus of Kermit-the-frog suits—I love that Kermit and don't know why more kids don't want to dress up like him—so I decided, if you come here in regular clothes, then poof, you turn into a frog! I only thought they were sending a dozen or so, but we've got at least fifty. And it's a good thing we've got them, too!" SpongeBob SquarePants and Frodo Baggins cleared out of the way as SBB continued down the stairs. "I don't see what the big deal is—people told me what to wear for the first twelve years of my life and I turned out just fine!"

I decided to sidestep that one. "So, who's needed them so far?"

"Mostly freshmen boys, it seems. Mmm, lot of mediums." Sara-Beth spotted a girl dressed as a skeleton. She tapped her on the shoulder angrily. "Do you have a problem with me?" she demanded. "Are you trying to say something about my weight?"

Everyone standing on the staircase stopped their

conversations to look at the girl. The girl, totally confused, scratched the bone appliqué on her elbow.

"No?" she offered hopefully. "I think you're cool."

"Okay, just checking," Sara-Beth said, cheerful again. She took my arm and we walked into the living room. "So, Flan, when you see this Adam, I want you to tell me right away, all right?"

"Sure. But don't talk about him anymore right now."

"Why n—oh, I see."

Meredith and Judith stood not too far away, over by the punch bowl. From the way they were scanning the crowd, I could tell neither of them had bumped into Adam yet. They looked kind of happy when they saw Sara-Beth Benny, though.

"Sara-Beth!" Judith ran up to her and they air-kissed. Meredith hung back, sipping her punch.

"Is he here yet?" she asked me in an undertone. But Sara-Beth has ears like a hawk, and apparently she heard, because she whirled around, all dramatic.

"Do you mean the mysterious quarterback I keep hearing rumors about?" she exclaimed. "Because I just realized, nobody's even told me what he looks like yet!"

"His face is so sensitive," Meredith cooed. "His eyes shine like starlight!"

"He's tall and handsome. Like a movie star," said Judith, frowning at her friend.

"He cuts a dashing figure," Meredith retorted. "In earlier times, he would've ridden horses across the moor."

"You don't even know what a moor is," Judith snapped. "Listen, he's hot. Really hot."

"Lots of guys are hot. Adam has a piercing gaze and the grace of an immortal."

Sara-Beth Benny looked utterly confused. So I put in, "He's got a bandage on his elbow. From where he scraped it in the football game."

"Oh!" she cried. "I remember him. He didn't have a costume either—so lame! And he's not an immortal or a movie star—he's just a frog."

Meredith and Judith looked at each other.

"I have to go to the bathroom," said Judith.

"I've got to check out your amazing new house," said Meredith.

And they took off in opposite directions, combing the room for frogs. Sara-Beth raised an eyebrow.

"I warned you," I said. "They're totally insane."

She shook her head, and I noticed for the first time the earrings she was wearing. They were little gold teeth.

"I do have to say, Flan," she said, snaking her bird-like arm around my waist, "you hang out with some of the strangest people."

*S*ara-Beth declared that she had to go mingle with her other guests. I felt badly pointing out that she didn't really know most of them, so I let her go alone, and a couple of minutes later I was all by myself, standing awkwardly in the middle of the living room, trying to avoid making eye contact with any of the Kermits. It was really disappointing that the party wasn't the small, intimate affair SBB and I had planned. It had seemed like such a great plan at the time. And I wished Bennett had been able to come. It seemed so much harder to remember that I didn't want to see Adam when Bennett wasn't by my side, reminding me what an amazing guy he was. Even though it was difficult to be around them with all the secrets I was keeping, I felt a little lonely since Meredith and Judith had ditched me, and I couldn't really go talk to anyone else, because I couldn't recognize my classmates in their costumes.

After a moment of feeling badly for myself, I went to the refreshments table, leaned over a tray full of caramel apples decorated to look like jack-o'-lanterns, and ladled out a cup of punch for myself. But some creepy guy dressed like one of the winged monkeys from *The Wizard of Oz* kept staring at me, so I wandered upstairs again, hoping to find somewhere quiet in one of the back rooms to just sit and figure stuff out.

Right after she moved in, Sara-Beth converted the bedroom at the end of the hall into a walk-in closet on a grand scale, with two giant chests of drawers and a couple of clothing racks stretching all the way from one wall to another. I went in and closed the door behind me. It was kind of comforting in there, with all the Prada and Versace and Chloé dresses rustling around, and the wall of shoes arranged by color, like one of those rainbow spectrums from science class. I sat on the window seat nearest the door and stared down into the yard. Sara-Beth's decorator had strung up a bunch of little paper lanterns shaped like skulls, and a big group of my classmates were out there in their costumes, chattering and mingling and moving around. They all looked so playful and friendly in their superhero capes, rubber masks, and bedsheet togas that I almost wanted to go down there and join them. But making new friends wouldn't solve the trouble with my current friends. I sighed, and the glass fogged up a little, so I wrote my initials in script in the steam like I used to do when I was little: F.F.

The door squeaked open, showing part of the hall-way and a figure silhouetted against the light. I sat up and tried to look cheerful. I didn't want some total stranger to think I was in here moping around because no one would talk to me. But when the guy came all the way into the room, I realized it wasn't a stranger at all. It was Adam.

"Hey," he said, lifting the Kermit-the-frog mask off his head. "I've been looking around for you for, like, ever. What're you doing hiding out in here?"

I'd been avoiding this exact moment all evening and the minute I was in it, my heart started beating faster in my chest. And I knew that, despite all the problems he was causing me and my friends, he was the one person I'd really wanted to see.

"Oh, you know . . . it was crowded," I stammered, feeling shy and kind of embarrassed to have been caught in SBB's *über*-closet.

He walked into the room, carrying the Kermit-the-frog mask under one arm like a football helmet. The green terry-cloth suit looked funny on him, like he was walking around in pajamas or something, and, despite all the guilt and nervousness I was feeling, I started to giggle.

"What?" he asked, sitting down next to me on the window seat.

"You look ridiculous in that costume."

"This?" Adam gestured at his fuzzy green ensemble and said in a mock-serious voice, "This is no costume. I think it's time you know—I'm Bogie's real father."

I laughed again, this time for real.

"Listen, I've been wanting to talk to you," he told me. "Someplace more private than the bio room. Because you never said anything about what happened after the game the other night. I mean I e-mailed you, but I never heard back. . . ." He trailed off.

I hadn't said anything because I didn't know what to say. And I still didn't.

"I wish I could say I just kissed you on impulse, but there's more to it than that," he went on. "It's something I've been wanting to do for a long time. I know we haven't known each other for long, but there's something about you—"

"But Adam . . ." My voice came out as a squeak, and I cleared my throat. "Adam, I have a boyfriend. You must know that."

"I do. That's what makes this so hard. I mean, I

hoped you were just friends when I saw you guys in the stairwell, but . . ." He looked down. "Bennett's a great guy—he's smart and funny and really . . . real. I can see why you like him so much. We've been e-mailing back and forth—and he mentioned you guys were dating—and so far, from everything he's said and done, he seems like a real stand-up guy. I keep thinking, if I'd met him any other time, under any other circumstances, we would've been friends." Adam moved his face close to mine. "But the way things are now, I can't talk to him without feeling jealous. Because of you."

It was funny: watching Adam from a distance, like on the football field or from across the room at a big high school party, he seems so confident and unbreakable. But talking right then, he looked so . . . I don't know, so vulnerable. When he was breaking everybody else's heart it was easy to forget that his own heart could get broken, too. So I guess that's why, when he leaned in to kiss me, I didn't stop him.

The minute it started happening, though, I knew it was wrong. I'd only kissed two guys before Adam—Bennett and my first boyfriend, Jonathan—so I had some idea how I wanted to feel during a kiss: safe and happy. But even though Adam was a good kisser—a really good kisser, actually—and totally adorable, I didn't feel that way at all. Instead, I felt guilty, nervous, and worried that someone might see us. And that pretty much takes all the fun out of a kiss.

I pulled away and looked past him, down the hall, and what made things even worse was that, the minute I did, I saw Judith sidling up to another lanky green frog, taking him by the hand, and standing on her tiptoes to push up his frog mask up past his lips to get a look at him. I looked away, out the window, and—there was Meredith, standing in a corner of the garden, deep in conversation with a frog of her own. I looked back at Adam, who was watching me, looking hurt and confused.

"What's wrong?" he asked.

I took a deep breath. "Adam, I really like you—I do—but I just can't do this."

"But Flan—"

"Like I said, I have a boyfriend . . . and . . . and it just doesn't feel right." I got up. "I have to go."

"Flan? Flan—wait!" But I was already out the door, taking off down the hall at top speed.

Chapter 27

*B*y the time I got out to the hallway, Judith and her frog had disappeared. I pushed through a bunch of kids dressed as jungle animals and flew past them down the stairs. Even over the noise of the party, I could still hear Adam calling me, but I ignored him and hurried away, holding on tight to the banister strung with bloodred Christmas tree lights.

I didn't see SBB, and couldn't figure out where to go, or what to do. I thought that maybe I could scramble over the garden wall back into my own yard, or at least sit down outside for a while and get a breath of fresh air, but I knew for sure that there was no way I could think straight in this room full of shouts and laughter and guys dressed like Gandalf, small-town sheriffs, and the balding Stuy principal, Mr. Skille. I was halfway through the living room, headed for the kitchen, when all of a

215

sudden I felt a hand on my shoulder. I turned around. Kermit.

"Listen, Adam," I hissed, "I'm serious! We can't keep doing this." I shook his hand off my shoulder. "Someone could see us."

Kermit stood still for a long moment, like he was some kind of puppet statue. Then he reached up and took his frog-head off.

I gasped. It wasn't Adam at all. It was Bennett, and he had this horrible look on his face, like I'd totally, totally betrayed him.

Which, I realized with a stabbing pain in my stomach, I had. I had been so worried about Meredith and Judith fighting, and about whether I liked Adam or Bennett more, that I had never really considered how hurt Bennett would be if he knew I had feelings for Adam.

My mouth was still hanging open and I was so startled I couldn't think straight. I just wanted to wipe that awful, hurt look off his face. But the first thing I managed to say was, "I thought you weren't coming!"

Bennett looked away. His eyes were already starting to get kind of wet-looking.

"Obviously," he croaked.

"No—wait, Bennett, that's not what I meant at all. I mean—" It was hard to get words to come out right with him staring at me like I'd just ripped up all his *Green Lantern*s.

"I can't believe you're cheating on me. And with Adam," he spat. "God, do I feel stupid. I actually thought I was becoming friends with him. And you . . . I can't even—" His voice cracked, and he turned to walk away from me.

"Bennett—Bennett!" I tried to grab on to his arm, but he took off into the crowd.

My classmates danced wildly around me, clearly having the times of their lives, but I stood motionless as a hollow, aching feeling crept over my body. My throat tightened, and I worried I was going to start crying right there in the middle of SBB's haunted living room. What had I done? Someone knocked into me, spilling bloodred punch on my beautiful dress, and I felt that the night couldn't get any worse . . . until I turned around and saw Meredith and Judith standing there, glaring fiercely at me. I never would've dreamed that a girl-pirate and a ladybug could be scary costumes, but right then they seemed like they'd come right out of one of those awful slasher movies.

"How long have you been there?" I gasped.

"Long enough," snapped Judith.

"I can't believe you, Flan." Meredith shook her

head in disbelief. "All that talk about saving our friendships and guys not being worth it, and this whole time you were—I mean, did you set the No Adam Rule just so you could keep him for yourself? Who would've thought you'd be the kind of person to do such a thing?"

"No, wait!" I cried, grabbing Judith's arm. "Listen, this is all just a big misunderstanding. I can explain everything."

Judith angrily shook my hand off. "We're sick of your explanations, Flan!"

"Yeah," Meredith put in. "What kind of friend steals a guy like that?"

"I wasn't stealing him, though!" I said pleadingly, desperate to make them understand. "I swear, he just kissed me—and—and I didn't know what to do."

"Yeah, right!" Judith put her hands on the hips of her ripped black pirate skirt. "He just kissed you out of the blue! Because he always goes around doing that. Puh-lease."

"Yeah," Meredith agreed. "If it was that easy to get him to kiss you, then I—then people'd be doing it all the time."

"He just likes me." Why did every word that tumbled out of my mouth just make things worse?

"Well, I don't see what's so special about you," said

Judith. "You don't even have on a sexy costume. Come on, Meredith." She grabbed her friend's arm and the two of them stalked off. She whirled around one last time and called back, "And Cinderella? Grow up, Flan."

I stared after them miserably, wishing I had a fairy godmother to wave her wand and make everything go back to the way it used to be.

I went to search for Bennett, hoping against hope that he hadn't left the party yet. I was worried he was out wandering the streets of New York in his borrowed, footie frog suit. The idea kind of broke my heart. But I tore around the party anyway, hoping to get a glimpse of a dejected Kermit so I could try to talk to him at least. I went into the kitchen, where a bunch of burly guys were having a Bloody Mary–drinking contest, then out into the backyard, where I ran into Philippa and Mickey. Philippa was lounging on a lawn chair wearing a black turtleneck dress, a black velvet cape, and red lipstick. She looked sophisticated and a little bit bored. Mickey, on the other hand, was wearing torn jeans and running around, shaking his head like a wet dog. Apparently he had fallen into the apple-bobbing tub and gotten his shirt completely drenched.

"Hey, Flan," Philippa called to me from over on her lawn chair, waving me over with her drink.

"Some party, huh, Flan?" a wild-eyed Mickey said with a wide grin. A piece of red apple skin was stuck to his front tooth, and his dark hair was all stringy and wet. It looked like the only part of him that had been washed in days. I couldn't decide if he was supposed to be Kurt Cobain, a lumberjack, or just a pile of dirty laundry. "How've you been? I haven't seen you or Patch since Feb lost her sense of humor."

"Tell me about it," I said. I was trying to keep my cool, but I guess I looked upset, because Philippa tilted her head at me, all concerned.

"Hey, Flan, is everything okay?" she asked.

"Well, I'm just looking around for my boyfriend, Bennett." As soon as I said the word *boyfriend,* I realized that it was probably no longer true. "Has he come through here? He's wearing a Kermit suit."

"I haven't seen him," said Philippa. "Mickey?"

"Hang on just a sec, there's my cell." After some groping around, Mickey found his phone in his pants pocket. "Hey, it's your brother!" He flipped open his phone. "Patch, you're back from the dead!"

"I don't think he's seen him," Philippa mouthed.

I nodded and wandered away before Mickey could think to put me on the phone with Patch. The last thing I wanted right then was to talk to my crazy family.

I went back inside to check the kitchen again and was about to give up the search when I suddenly spotted Bennett coming up from the door that led to SBB's basement. He'd taken off his Kermit costume and was wearing some sort of stained, torn green suit with a V across the front of it and moon boots splattered with what looked like raw fruit. I rushed up to him.

"Bennett, listen, I'm so sorry," I panted. "I know this looks bad, but just give me a chance to explain, please?"

"Leave me alone, Flan. I'm going home," he muttered.

"But Bennett, I just want to explain!"

"I don't want to hear it. It's obvious what happened—I don't need the details." He pushed past me and started down the hall, but I caught up with him again when he ran into a group of former United States presidents.

"Well, at least tell me what happened to your clothes? And why aren't you baby-sitting your cousin?" I asked, squeezing past Abe Lincoln.

"I was never going to baby-sit my cousin," he shot back. "I just wanted to surprise you."

"Surprise me?" I repeated, baffled.

"You were so upset about your frog dissection unit, I wanted to help you." He barked out a sharp laugh. "So I've been at Stuyvesant with my brother all night, rescuing the frogs out of your bio classroom so he could take them all upstate to the nature preserve he works at on the weekends."

"Oh my God. I can't believe you did that." I wanted to reach out to hug him, but he was looking at me with such a disgusted expression that I let my arms fall limp at my sides.

"Yeah, well, it seemed important to you. Afterward I put on this Buck Rogers costume—remember, that old comic book space hero from the movie we watched at your house? No, of course you don't—you were probably daydreaming about third downs or whatever the whole time."

"I was not!" I protested. The fact was, though, I *had* kind of tuned out most of the movie. When I told Bennett I loved old films from the '40s, he apparently thought that meant I liked guys who talked like radio announcers and dressed like rejects from the starship *Enterprise*, when what I really liked were towering romances and vintage Chanel ball gowns. Bennett had made the movie even more boring by constantly pausing it to talk about how it was different from the "groundbreaking" comic book series, the first four books of which he'd found on microfiche at the library. I tried to think of something that would prove I'd been paying attention. "There was a girl astronaut in it who wore an aviator cap, wasn't there?"

He went on as if he hadn't heard me. "But when I cut through the parade to get here, I wound up getting pulled onto this float covered with people dressed up as angry gorillas, and well . . ." He looked down at his ruined costume.

"Oh, Bennett," I said.

"When I got here I got sent down to the basement by some guy named Thorn, and it was the weirdest thing I've ever seen in my life: all these rusted chains and iron shackles were hanging on the walls of the stairs. Down at the bottom, this guy done up as some sort of leather Viking shoved me in a frog suit." His eye flashed angrily. "You know the rest."

I blurted out. "Bennett, I know you're mad—and you have every right to be—but if we could just talk about it—"

"Mad? That's a huge understatement. Flan, this has been the worst night of my life. I think I'll exercise my 'right' to be 'mad' somewhere really far away from you." And with that, he stormed out of the party, the door loudly slamming shut behind him.

I was sitting in the upstairs guest room on the patchy black velvet cushions of an ancient sofa, crying, when Sara-Beth Benny flitted into the room. She may not have been a fairy godmother, but there was no one in the world I wanted to see more.

"Sweetness, I just heard," she said, flinging her bony arms around me. She sat down on the couch. "I could kill that boy—he's absolutely ruined the party. I mean of course no one noticed but I just can't believe anyone would talk to you that way."

"But I deserved it." I sniffled. "I'm a terrible person, Sara-Beth. I've messed everything up tonight."

"Don't say things like that!" She looked shocked. "Flan, this is all a question of bad luck and bad timing. No jury in the world would convict you, and with all the courtroom dramas I've been in, I should know."

"I'm not saying I should go to jail." I blew my nose into one of the black napkins with fanged purple spiders on them from a stack Sara-Beth Benny had handed me. "But I've been a lousy friend and an even worse girlfriend."

Sara-Beth shook her head. "Everyone makes mistakes, Flan. Think of how many times I've decorated this place in absolutely hideous styles! There was the Moroccan nightmare, the life pod, the 1960s bubble furniture, the French country—"

I blinked away some of my tears. "Bubble furniture? I don't remember that."

"Oh, you must not have been here that day." She sighed. "But anyway, my point is, if people couldn't make mistakes and change their minds, we'd be sitting on floor pillows right now, surrounded by bronze elephants, and quite frankly that's one of the last things I need in my life. Now listen." She seized my hands in hers. "All I want in the world is for you to relax and enjoy yourself. Please, please, please don't let this party become the party where my best friend has a nervous breakdown! I've had too many parties like that already."

I nodded. "I'm sorry, Sara-Beth."

"There's no reason to apologize to me! I just want to see you smile."

I smiled weakly, and Sara-Beth clapped her hands. She's such a funny girl: she'll fill her house with spiderwebs, taxidermied kittens, and rotting Victorian furniture, but she's got pretty good sense when it comes to cheering me up.

"Okay," I told her, drying my eyes. "I'm going to go talk to Meredith and Judith. I think I'll feel a lot better if they don't hate me, at least."

"Hooray! And I know just where they are, too."

For the party, Sara-Beth's decorator had hung heavy black curtains over her guest bedroom's windows; the only light in the room came from pinpricks in the fabric that were patterned to look like spooky constellations—an octopus, a UFO, a skull. A bunch of kids were sitting on the floor by the bed, sticking their hands into bowls filled with food designed to feel disgusting and scary. When Sara-Beth and I went in, everyone groaned and covered their eyes at the light from the hallway.

"Ew! Peeled grapes," Sara-Beth shrieked, plunging her hand into the nearest container. "They're so gross and sticky! Don't they feel like eyeballs or something?"

As my eyes adjusted to the darkness, I noticed Meredith and Judith, leaning against the taxidermied carcass of a grinning wolf. They were glaring at me.

Between them sat the bowl of spaghetti I'd abandoned on the snake cage earlier in the evening.

"Hey," I said, feeling weird and shy. "Mind if I sit here?"

They kept scowling at me, but they didn't say no, so I sank down near them on the blue furry-monster carpet.

"I really need to talk to you guys," I said in an undertone.

"Dried apricots!" Sara-Beth was shrieking. "They're all shriveled!"

"Somewhere quieter," I added.

"Who says we want to talk to you?" Judith still sounded snippy, but not nearly as mad as she had earlier. I decided to take this as a good sign.

"I don't know if you guys want to talk to me or not, but I really want to talk to you. Come on, please?" I gave them my best beseeching look, which wasn't too hard—I really didn't know what I'd do if they wouldn't hear me out. "Please? You can hate me again as soon as I'm finished, I promise."

Meredith and Judith looked at each other. Meredith shrugged. Judith sighed.

"Okay, okay," she muttered. The three of us got up and left the room.

Out in the hallway, Judith folded her arms. "So what's your explanation?"

I bit my lip. It suddenly occurred to me that even though I'd dragged them out here, I still had no idea what to say.

"You totally, totally have the right to be mad at me. Furious even." I took a deep breath. "I'm furious with myself. But I just can't stand the thought of losing your friendship over this. You both mean more to me than any guy ever could." Meredith and Judith glanced at each other doubtfully.

"If that's true, then why did you kiss him?" Meredith asked accusingly. "Didn't you make us promise not to go after him just so you could have him for yourself?"

I shook my head. "I know you have no reason to believe me, but I swear I didn't. I didn't even think I liked him then. At first he just seemed like this random jock, and I thought you were crazy to let him come between you. Then I got to know him a little better—in bio class and stuff—and I started to see what you both liked about him. I didn't tell you because I thought I could just keep the feelings stuffed down inside— I honestly never dreamed anything would happen between us." My voice started to crack. "And I really regret that it did. I'm so stupid sometimes."

"I just can't believe you'd act like this, Flan." Judith was still scowling.

"I seriously screwed up. But you guys mean the world to me. I can't imagine Stuy without you. And that's the truth." I took a deep breath. "I think we all let the Adam situation mess with our judgment."

Judith puffed herself up. "No, we didn't! At least not the way you did."

But Meredith just looked down at her shoes.

"Judith, I have something I have to tell you," she admitted. "Earlier, when we all split up . . . well, I wasn't really exploring the house. I was looking for Adam. And when I got outside, I finally found him."

"You did?" Judith turned bright red with anger. "You kissed Adam too?"

"Well . . . not exactly. See, there was this guy in a Kermit suit, and something about him—the way he was standing by himself, all *contemplative*, you know—I thought it was Adam. So I started flirting with him. I quoted some poetry and stuff, and told him about how I've liked him for a long, long time. He seemed really thrilled—almost like no one had ever said that stuff to him before. I kissed him, but when he took off his Kermit head . . ." She hesitated. "Well, it turns out it was Jules. I was so embarrassed, I didn't know how to tell him I'd mixed him up with someone else. So . . ." She smiled timidly. "We're going to the movies on Friday."

Judith looked flustered. "I can't believe you'd do something like that, Meredith."

Meredith shrugged sheepishly.

At that point, a whole series of weird expressions crossed over Judith's face. One of them was this sort of nasty, smug expression, like she was about to launch into some long, dramatic thing about how she was oh so morally superior to her backstabbing friends. But the other expression was something I'd never seen on her face before, a kind of terrible, contorted frown. Finally, the second face won.

"Okay, I have to tell you guys something," she exploded, "but you have to promise not to laugh. Okay?"

Meredith and I nodded.

"When I went off to go to the bathroom, I was look-ing for Adam too. And I thought I finally found him in the upstairs hallway, because this frog looked kind of tall and football-playerish. So I was being all flirty and touching his arm, and I even made some horrible pun about 'pirate's booty' . . . I almost couldn't believe it, but he seemed totally into it and said, 'I guess you like me,' and I was like, 'I can't know if I like a guy until he kisses me,' and then I kissed him. But when he took off his Kermit head—" She covered her face with her hands. "Oh, I just can't tell you, it's way too embarrassing."

"Tell us!" Meredith and I both shrieked.

Judith slowly lowered her hands from her face. "It was Kelvin!" she whispered.

Meredith and I immediately broke our promise and started laughing hysterically, and after a long moment, Judith did too.

"But in art class he was building a Jar Jar Binks mask! You know, from *Star Wars*!" Meredith exclaimed. "What happened?"

Judith threw up her hands. "Yeah, apparently some mariachi band bumped into him when he was getting on the A train and the giant head got crushed in the subway doors."

Meredith started laughing again, but I just frowned. As funny as it was to picture Kelvin with his alien head stuck in the doors of a subway car, it reminded me a little too much of what Bennett had gone through earlier.

"At least you know you can hit on guys you like now," said Meredith. "It just sucks that it was Kelvin this time. Of all the guys at the party to randomly flirt with . . ."

"Tell me about it. It was sooo embarrassing," Judith said. "I don't know if I can stand to face him in bio next week."

"Maybe Mr. Phelps'll let you switch lab partners,"

Meredith suggested. "Or you could tell him you'd rather just work alone."

I thought of Adam and wondered if I could switch, too. But I knew I wouldn't even ask. It would hurt Adam's feelings way too much if I skipped out on him before we finished the amphibian life unit. Of course, now that Bennett and his brother had taken off with all the frogs, maybe the unit would be over. Everything was such a mess. But at least I was here now, hanging out with my friends at an awesome party. I just needed to concentrate on that for a while.

"Listen," I said, "I'm just glad we're not all tearing each others' eyes out. I don't think I could take it if you both stayed mad at me for much longer. I know I messed up badly, but being friends with you really means a lot to me."

Meredith and Judith nodded. They looked like they knew what I meant.

"I have an idea," said Meredith. "How about we make a new pinky promise?"

"Oh no, here we go again," Judith groaned.

"No, let's not make any more rules about guys. That obviously doesn't work. I don't think you can stop yourself from liking someone anyway." Meredith stuck her pinky finger out at us—it was painted with black and red ladybug polka dots. "Let's promise instead we'll all work on being better friends. Nicer, more honest, the works. And let's promise to always remember that, even when cute guys are around."

I nodded. "That sounds good to me."

"All right," Judith agreed.

So we linked pinkies and swore on it. And even if it was kind of a silly, little-kid thing to do, I had a feeling we would all keep our promise this time.

Chapter 30

*M*eredith and Judith were both supposed to be home by midnight, but I was in no big hurry to go back to my house to face Feb, who had probably worked herself into some kind of homicidal rage by this point in the evening. So after they took off, I stuck around at Sara-Beth Benny's.

The last party guests trailed out around two-thirty in the morning, wigs on backward, masks in hand, and by then I was totally exhausted. Sara-Beth announced that she was calling a cleaner in the morning, but I still felt like I should help her get the place in some kind of order before I just took off. The place was an absolute mess: half-empty cups of punch sat on all the shelves, tables, and faux-coffin lids; and cookie crumbs, spilled spaghetti, and peeled grapes splattered the already-musty carpets. Plus, a lot of people had taken off parts of their costumes, so random accessories were all over the place: a feather boa on the mantelpiece, fake nails by the bathroom sink, stage blood, and a rubber arm stump under the couch.

"I'm sorry everybody trashed your house, Sara-Beth," I said, dragging a black garbage bag around the living room and dropping cups, apple cores, and crumpled napkins into it. "It was a great party, though."

"Wasn't it?" Sara-Beth flung herself into a decaying armchair with carved claw feet. Dust rose up out of the ancient cushions. "The only thing I'm sorry about is that it's over. The house looked absolutely gorgeous, don't you think?"

I carefully extracted a paper plate from behind a taxidermied raven. As odd and musty as the haunted décor was, of all the styles she'd tried, it really was the one that most suited the house—and her. "Maybe you should just keep it this way," I joked.

Sara-Beth's eyes widened, and she leapt out of her dusty chair. "Flan, that's an amazing idea," she gasped. "I can't believe I didn't think of it myself! Oh, this is so exciting! I'll have a haunted house forever. I can just see it now," she went on excitedly. "I can buy old angels from cemeteries and put them in the backyard. And I'll put a creaky old iron gate out front, with spikes and gargoyles on it, and hang Day of the Dead marionette skeletons in the upstairs windows. Maybe

I can even get some of those paintings where the eyes follow you back and forth! And I'll need to get a hologram machine, of course. Trick mirrors . . . Think of all the places I'll have to hide from the paparazzi! This is so fantastic, Flan! You're such a good friend. You know me better than I know myself!"

I pulled a maroon wig with bangs out from behind some yellowing lace pillows on the Victorian settee and smiled to myself. Sara-Beth was wrong—even after all the time we'd spent together, she always managed to surprise me. But she was right about the haunted house—it was kooky, cute, and a little bit overwhelming (in a good way), just like she was.

Sara-Beth sank back into the chair with a satisfied sigh, and curled her legs underneath her like she was a very thin, very tall black cat. "So tell me what happened with Meredith and Judith. Did Bennett ever come back and make up for the horrible, horrible way he treated you?"

"I'm the one who needs to apologize, but he won't even talk to me." I rubbed my eyes tiredly. Thinking of Bennett turned my insides into one big guilty tangle. "Meredith and Judith don't hate me anymore, but he totally does. And he probably should, after what I did."

"Don't be silly!" Sara-Beth waved her arms, releasing

more dust from the chair cushions. "Bennett's a nice guy, but you deserve so much better. Any boy too lame to wear a costume on Halloween is way too lame for my Flan."

Thinking of Bennett saving Bogie and then getting trampled in the parade after all the time he'd taken to get his costume ready made me want to cry. I threw the lint-covered paper towel I'd been dusting with into the trash bag and flopped down on top of the cold, hard marble coffin in the center of the room. "I've made such a mess of everything, Sara-Beth. What do you think I should do? Call him? Beg for forgiveness? Just give him some space? I just know he's going to hate me forever."

Sara-Beth came over and perched next to me on the coffin. "Shh," she soothed, putting her arm around me. I noticed she was wearing fake black nails that pointed at the tip. "It's all going to be fine. And if he hates you forever, well, that's his loss. You're a wonderful person. So you made one mistake, but you didn't set out to hurt him." She looked darkly at the wall. "Unlike certain people I've known, who think it's so much fun to tell Conan O'Brien that we were never going out, when everyone knows we had a deep spiritual connection!" Sara-Beth took a deep breath. "Anyway, my point is, you did the best you could, under the circumstances.

It's not your fault that you like Adam better! That's why we have dating instead of some crazy system of arranged marriages that's based on, like, how many goats a guy has. The whole point is to find the person you like the most before you get stuck with some lunatic who tries to control your spending!"

"Yeah, but I'm still not sure." I dabbed at my eyes with the stained skirt of my princess dress. "I think Adam may just be a crush. He's more of a guy's guy, while Bennett's sweet and smart and understands me. But then again Adam . . ." I trailed off. "I just wish I knew what would make me happy."

"Well, there's no reason to get all worked up about it now," Sara-Beth pointed out. "Before my mom and I split up, she always used to say this great thing: 'If it's meant to be, there's always tomorrow.'"

"Tomorrow?" I repeated.

"Yes! In the morning, this'll all seem a lot less complicated, I promise. And there's nothing so urgent that can't wait till then." Sara-Beth yawned. "Everything makes sooo much more sense after a full night of sleep."

I nodded. "Speaking of which, I'd better be getting home."

"You're sure you don't want to stay over? There's a bed in the guest room shaped like a Venus flytrap, and it's super comfy." Her forehead wrinkled. "Almost *too* comfy."

"I think Feb will freak if I don't come home." I hopped down off the coffin onto the floor, landing near the bloody chalk outline of the murdered SBB. "But maybe we can get breakfast in the morning or something."

Then I groaned and smacked my forehead. I'd completely forgotten it was a school night, and the thought of dragging myself out of bed in less than four hours only to face Bennett and Adam seemed even less appealing than spending the night in a Venus flytrap. "Ugg. School. I think I might have to take a sick day. That is, if Feb'll let me."

Sara-Beth walked me to the door and I crept down the sidewalk toward my house. I had a big decision ahead of me, boyfriend-wise, but SBB was right—right now I just needed to get home and make it to bed.

Already I was dreading the prospect of a fight with Feb. I was way too exhausted for any more drama tonight, and the last thing I needed was another person screaming at me for all the stuff I'd done wrong. When I walked up the steps to our door, though, I noticed something weird. Not only were all the lights on—that could've just meant that Feb was waiting up for me, wearing an apron and holding a rolling pin like she was planning on hitting me with it—but music was playing loud enough that I could hear the beat through the closed windows. It was blasting, actually. And pieces of smashed pumpkin pulp were splattered all over the sidewalk out front. What was the deal? Nervously, I started to put my key in the lock. Then I realized the door was already open. As it swung inside on its hinges, I was so surprised by what I saw that I almost fell backward down the steps.

Chapter 31

I FACE THE MUSIC

My house looked like a bomb had exploded right in the middle of it. A disco ball dangled crookedly from the light fixture in the living room; half-empty boxes of pizza lay on the floor; Pabst Blue Ribbon cans sat on the bookcase, the top of the TV, and the back of the sofa. One crunched under my Lucite-clad foot as I stepped inside.

The noise almost knocked me over—a guy dressed as Marilyn Manson was standing at the top of the stairs accompanying the already deafening music bursting from our stereo speakers on his trombone. I figured Noodles was upstairs somewhere, probably hiding out under my bed in terror, barking frantically like he'd completely lost his mind.

And I couldn't believe the sheer number of people packed into our downstairs. Philippa was chasing a now-shirtless Mickey around a corner into the hallway;

242

David, one of my brother's oldest friends, was pouring a pumpkin-colored drink from a cocktail shaker into a juice glass, and Liesel and her ex-boyfriend, Arno, were snuggling together in our brown leather chair like nothing had ever kept them apart. And there was Patch, looking more like himself he had all week, sipping a beer and nodding at a tan surfer-type guy, who was talking emphatically and making wave-like motions with his hands. Plus, there were about a million people all over the place I'd never seen before in my life: a girl with raccoon eyes and a tight Prada dress waving around a Chinatown kite shaped like a fish; a guy with asymmetrical hair and an eyebrow ring doing the funky chicken by himself; a six-foot-tall woman dressed up as a glittery cowgirl in five-inch heels, fake eyelashes, and a cowboy hat made entirely of sequins.

But through all the chaos my eyes latched onto the most shocking sight in the room: Feb, wearing a bronze, metal-plated Roberto Cavalli dress and black Jimmy Choo stilettos, dancing wildly on the coffee table.

I must've stood there in front of the wide open door for a full minute before Liesel noticed I was there and tried to shout hello over the din. Then there was a kind of ripple effect around the room, and it seemed like pretty much everyone turned around at the same time and screamed, "Hi, Flan!"

For a moment I felt stunned, but all of a sudden I felt really, really martini-glass-throwing mad. I had been going crazy dealing with Feb's insane overprotectiveness, and then she turned around and threw a huge party the minute I was out of the house? And on a precious "school night," no less. I slammed the door shut behind me, then, pushing past a couple wearing togas and laurel leaves, shouldered my way up to the middle of the living room.

"Hey, Feb!" I yelled, tugging at her heavy skirt. It felt like chain mail.

"Flanny!" she shrieked exuberantly, jumping off the table like she was wearing sneakers instead of skinny heels. "I'm so glad you're here."

"What's going on?" I demanded as the aqua fish kite sailed over my head.

Feb clapped her hand over her mouth. "Oh no, you're mad at me. Don't be mad, Flanny! What happened was Liesel and Philippa and Mickey were at Sara-Beth's Halloween party—which I was not invited to, by the way—but apparently the place was swarming with all these loser Kermits. So, anyway, Patch told them they could come on over here, and then they invited their friends, and their friends invited their friends, and, well . . ." She flung her glitter-covered arms out and teetered slightly on her heels.

I crossed my arms and scowled at her, although it's hard to stay mad at Feb when she's in a good mood.

"Oh, Flan," she said, dropping her arms again. "I'm so sorry I've been so terrible these last couple weeks."

"Umm . . ." What was I supposed to say? *No, you haven't been? It's okay?* "Does this mean you're going to stop now?"

Feb laughed loudly and ruffled my hair. "I quit my internship."

"You did? Really?"

"Yeah! My friend came back from her sick leave, and I was like, sayonara." February almost knocked my tiara off my head as she waved good-bye to the imaginary law firm. "Whoops." She giggled. "Seriously, though, the minute I walked out those doors, I was like, I am so never going to do that again. Or anything like it. They trick you into thinking it's the real world with the fluorescent lights and the paper cuts and the alphabetizing you can never get straight. But I just kind of wilted in there."

I started to smile a little. Feb had a special, very annoying way of "wilting."

"Which got me thinking—I don't want you wilting, Flan. I really don't. I mean, I ran out of that law firm so fast I broke my heel, and I don't want you running away from me like that." Her big blue eyes started to look a little watery.

I looked around the disaster that had become our living room and thought about her grounding me, making me come home after school, and being impossible to talk to during a week when I really could have used a big sister. Then I did something that surprised even me: I gave her a big hug.

Feb squeezed me back, then held me out at arm's length. "I don't know what I was so worried about— you're practically all grown up!"

"I don't know about that," I said, looking down sheepishly at my princess dress.

"I said practically. Hey—Mom and Dad came back early from their trip!"

I almost jumped a mile. "They did? Where are they?" I looked over my shoulder, like they might be wearing lampshades and swing dancing behind the couch.

Feb scrunched up her forehead. "Well, they had to go up to Quebec for this benefit dinner for some iodine deficiency thing, but they're definitely coming back sometime soon . . . I think. They were only here for like an hour. Mom needed to grab some shoes."

"Great." I sighed.

"Hey, don't look so glum, kiddo! They left us gift certificates for that new manicure shop down the street. We'll go tomorrow! Besides, when the cat's away . . ." She grabbed me by the hand. "Come on."

"Feb . . ."

But it was too late: she was pulling me up onto the coffee table with her, and with everyone partying and cheering all around us, I really had no choice but to dance.

"Oh, I totally forgot," she yelled. "There's some guy here who's been waiting around to talk to you all night!"

"Where?" I whirled around and there was Adam, sitting quietly on a side chair that he was much too big for, and he had Noodles in his lap, and Noodles was fast asleep. He got up and handed Noodles to Philippa, and I could see that he just couldn't stop smiling. Then all he did was walk over to me and say, "Hey, can we talk when you're finished dancing?"

"Sure—" But of course, right then Feb thought it'd be the funniest thing in the world to push me off the coffee table with her hip. I screamed and went up into the air and then fell right into Adam's arms.

"Feb!" I yelled.

"Well, somebody had to do it!" she screamed as she pulled a bunch of other kids onto the table.

"Are you okay?" Adam asked. I had my arms around his neck, and I kicked off my heels. They landed in a potted plant past the couch, and I just sighed.

"Way, way better than okay," I said.

For an Inside Girl,
life isn't always so sweet.

Find out what happens next in *Some Kind of Wonderful,* an Inside Girl novel by J. Minter

Still recovering from a disastrous Halloween party at Sara-Beth Benny's house and a short-lived but way-annoying phase when older sister Feb decided to be responsible, Flan Flood is through with romance, and she is hoping to prove to her friends that they mean more to her than any boy. But her old flame Bennett is still lingering in the background, and Adam, the gorgeous quarterback, is as sweet and cute as ever. In this third installment of the Inside Girl series, can Flan Flood stay true-blue to her friends, or will the love bug bite again?

Learn more about Flan and the Inside Girls at
www.insidegirlbooks.com

Find out how it all began in
the Insiders series, also by J. Minter

"The Insiders are *the* guys to watch. But if you fall
in love with them, get in line, right behind ME!"
—Zoey Dean, author of *The A-List*

For more info on the guys, visit
www.insidersbook.com

Wish you could choose a boyfriend as cute as Flan's?

Check out the new series
date him or dump him?
by Cylin Busby

With more than twenty possible endings
in each book, if he's not the boy of your
dreams, you can always go back
and choose another one!